VIKING ❋ QUEST book three

THE
INVISIBLE
FRIEND

LOIS WALFRID JOHNSON

MOODY PUBLISHERS
CHICAGO

© 2004 by
LOIS WALFRID JOHNSON

Aurland, Norway, is a real place filled with warmhearted people. The decision made by the *ting* at the end of this book is based on an historic precedent. However, the characters in this book are fictitious. Any resemblance to people living or dead is coincidental.

All Scripture quotations, unless otherwise indicated, are taken from the *Holy Bible, New Living Translation,* copyright © 1996. Used by permission of Tyndale House Publishers, Inc., Wheaton, Illinois 60189, U.S.A. All rights reserved.

Published in association with the literary agency of Alive Communications, Inc., 7680 Goddard Street, Suite 200, Colorado Springs, Colorado 80920.

Library of Congress Cataloging-in-Publication Data

Johnson, Lois Walfrid.
    The invisible friend / Lois Walfrid Johnson.
        p. cm. — (Viking quest ; 3)
    Summary: Briana O'Toole arrives in Norway to face her new life as a slave, all the while praying that God will send her brother, still in Ireland, to buy her freedom.
    ISBN 0-8024-3114-3
        1. Vikings—Juvenile fiction. [1. Vikings—Fiction. 2. Slaves—Fiction. 3. Christian life—Fiction. 4. Norway—History—To 1030—Fiction.] I. Title.

PZ7.J63255In 2004
[Fic]--dc22

                                                                2004001136

1 3 5 7 9 10 8 6 4 2

Printed in the United States of America

*Courage comes
in many sizes, shapes,
and forms.*

*Thank you, Roy,
for the kind of courage
that sets others free.*

CONTENTS

Introduction   9

1. The Outlaw Goat   11

2. Mikkel's Secret   23

3. Big Brother   31

4. Hayloft Hideaway   43

5. Secret Message   51

6. Gna!   63

7. Brown Robe   71

8. The Talking Cow   75

9. Daughter of the King   85

10. Lost Forever?   93

11. Dev's Surprise   97

12. Bree's Biggest Fear   109

13. Hacksilver!   119
14. A Matter of Trust   127
15. A Place Apart   135
16. Christmas Morning   147
17. The Storyteller   159
18. Troublemaker   163
19. The Reindeer Runs   177
20. On Trial   189
21. Slave or Free?   203
    Acknowledgments   211

INTRODUCTION

Deep in the fjords of Norway, the village of Aurland is an awesome place because of its natural beauty. Yet no matter where or when we live, there is a gift that is crucial to life itself. That gift is freedom.

If we have freedom, we often take it for granted. If we do not have freedom, it becomes more important than the air we breathe. What does it mean to be truly free? And what is freedom of the heart?

ONE

THE OUTLAW GOAT

A sudden gust of wind whipped between the mountains, lashed the water into waves, and caught Briana
O'Toole's reddish blonde hair. With one quick motion Bree
swept it out of her eyes and turned to face her new life.

Just then a swell of waves lifted the end of the Viking
ship as it rested on the shore. Moments before, this ship
that brought Bree from Ireland had sailed through a long,
narrow waterway to this settlement in the mountains. Now
sunlight shone on a waterfall spilling over a high rock wall.

Then the sun shone on the blonde hair of a tall woman
standing beside the water. Seeming to forget everything
else, Bree's enemy, Mikkel, leaned forward.

The moment the Viking ship touched shore, he

leaped over the side. By the time he touched the ground, the tall woman stood before him.

Mikkel straightened to his full height and tipped his head in respect. "Mamma," he said.

"Son," she answered. A tear slid down her cheek. "You were gone so long; I was afraid."

"I know. But I am here." Relief filled Mikkel's voice. "I am home."

A flash of envy, then anger, filled Bree's insides. *Home!* she wanted to spit out. *Mikkel is home, but I am not!* On a summer morning late in the tenth century, Mikkel had planned the raid that brought Bree and others from Ireland to the Aurland Fjord. Sometimes Bree wished Mikkel could be a friend. Other times she felt angry about everything he did.

As Viking sailors set down the ramp, Bree looked into the crowd gathered to meet the ship. There she saw a girl with sandy colored hair, brown eyes, and a dusting of freckles across her nose.

Who is she? Bree wondered. *Why do I think she's someone I know?*

The girl looked too thin, as if she had been sick. Yet she had to be at least eleven, perhaps twelve. As people streamed off the ship, Bree lost sight of her. Then far up on shore, Bree saw her again.

A long single braid hung down on the girl's shoulder. When she tossed it aside, her eyes lit with laughter. Bree knew that motion, that look of poking fun at something serious. *Could it possibly be?*

Across the distance their gaze met. The girl's mouth formed a round O, a gasp of recognition. The surprise of it shook Bree to the center of her being. *It's my sister Keely!*

One year younger than Bree, the two had been close friends as well as sisters. Then six years ago Vikings raided the monastery near their home in Ireland and stole Keely away. In a similar way, a more recent raid had brought Bree on a Viking longship to this fjord.

Filled with excitement, Bree pushed her way toward the side of the ship. *Maybe there's a reason I was captured by Vikings. Maybe something good will come out of it.*

In that instant of hope Bree could see herself bringing Keely home to their family. She could imagine Daddy and Mam and each of her brothers and sisters hugging and kissing Keely. Tears would come to their eyes and stream down their cheeks.

Keely! Yes, it has to be her!

But the girl turned away. A tall Viking stepped in front of Bree, blocking her view. Filled with panic, Bree tried to get around him. By the time she reached the side of the ship, the girl was gone.

Bree felt sick with disappointment. *It was Keely,* she thought. *I know it was Keely! But if it was, why did she turn away? Why did she act as if she doesn't know me?*

I'll find her, Bree promised herself. *And somehow we'll escape together!*

In the next moment, Mikkel turned away from his mother to face the Irish captives.

"Stop!" he called out. When two Irishmen pretended they did not understand, Mikkel held up both hands. "Wait!"

Instantly other Viking sailors formed a line across the shore. No Irish prisoner would pass through that line until the men told that person where to go.

In despair Bree looked around. Here, where the ship had landed, rock walls gave way to a valley. Green fields lined the river flowing through that valley. Close to the river was a line of houses. But nowhere could Bree see the girl she believed to be Keely.

Now, like it or not, Bree needed to begin her new life. But first she wanted to say good-bye to the Irish friends she had made on board ship.

Standing to one side, Bree looked for them. When Lil came near, Bree caught her new friend in a hug. "Courage to win," Bree whispered.

As Lil's gaze met hers, Bree felt a shock of surprise. Only two weeks before, this younger girl had been afraid of her own shadow. Now Lil lifted her head and crossed her arms on her chest in their secret sign. "Courage to win, Bree," she said softly.

"Wherever you are, you will be all right," Bree whispered.

"I know." Lil's eyes shone. "And you also."

Bree swallowed hard. "Mikkel said I'll be his mother's slave. I'll watch where you go. We'll find each other."

When they walked down the ramp, Lil was ahead of Bree. Mikkel motioned Lil toward a sturdy woman with kind blue eyes. Standing there, Bree watched to see what happened with each of her special friends.

As a girl growing up in Ireland, she had always longed to travel. Often she had climbed the mountain near her home to gaze through the mists and wonder what lay beyond the Irish Sea. Yet in the days since leaving Ireland, Bree had begun dreaming about her new quest—being home again with her family.

Again she thought of her sister Keely, of walking up to their cottage, opening the door, and shouting, "Surprise!"

Again Bree let herself hope. *If Dev comes, and Keely is here*—

Ever since being captured—since watching Mikkel release her fourteen-year-old brother, Devin, on a shore in northern Ireland, Bree had clung to one hope. One year older than Bree, Dev had always watched out for her. If Dev could, he'd be here now, a bag of ransom money in his hand. When Mikkel boasted about his father being chieftain of the Aurland Fjord, Dev had learned how to find Bree.

But now a tall slender girl headed toward Mikkel. Like many of the people standing on shore, she was also blonde, but her long thick hair fell down her back, nearly reaching her waist.

As she swept forward like a queen before her subjects, the girl's gaze went from one Irish person to the next, and then stopped on Bree.

The girl turned toward Mikkel. "Who is this?" she asked, her voice sharp.

"Well, *Gee-nah*," Mikkel drawled. "What a way to welcome me home."

But the girl named Gna paid no attention. "Who is she?" she asked again.

Mikkel looked uncomfortable but only said, "One of the Irish."

Stepping forward, Gna reached out her hand and tipped up Bree's chin with one finger. Bree backed away.

The girl followed, saying, "Look at me!"

Bree lifted her chin, but the girl's finger stayed beneath it. Bree had all she could do to keep herself from opening her mouth and snapping her teeth around the finger. If she had her way, the girl would be hollering with pain.

Instead, Bree opened her eyes wide. Without blinking, she stared at the girl with her meanest look. The girl stared back.

Mikkel laughed. "You've met your match, Gna. You can't beat her down."

"No?" Gna turned on him, and the coldness in her eyes became a fire in her face. "You think I can't. I've never known a person who hasn't learned to bow before me."

Bow? Bree asked herself, then realized she had spoken aloud.

Gna whirled on her. "So you know my language too. You will do more than bow. You will grovel in the dust of the earth before I am through with you. You will be my slave!"

Bree straightened, threw back her shoulders, and lifted her head. With the same movement, she turned slightly from looking at Gna to Mikkel. No words passed between Bree and Mikkel, but in that moment Bree knew he remembered.

"No, she won't," Mikkel said.

Gna stared at him. Even Bree felt surprised at the strength in his voice, but it was Gna who spoke. "You think not?"

A flush of embarrassment crept into Mikkel's neck, then into his face. But when he met Gna's gaze, there was no backing down. "She will not be your slave. She will be my mother's slave."

Gna laughed. The hard, cold sound of it sent a shiver down Bree's spine. Then to her surprise she forgot everything else. The bleating of sheep and bawling of cattle drowned out the voices of families on the beach.

As Bree swung around, she saw a wide, flat-bottomed boat that looked like a raft. The minute it came to rest on shore, the animals started over the low sides. A large billy goat led the rest. The billy headed straight for Gna.

"Gna!" Mikkel called in warning.

Whirling around, the girl saw her danger. Fingers spread wide, she held out her hands to stop him. His eyes focused on her, the goat kept coming. When Gna side-stepped to the right, he moved with her. When she leaped to the left, he followed.

"Help!" Gna cried, but to Bree's surprise, Mikkel stood as still as a rock.

Gna whirled on him. "Get that goat!" she commanded. In the moment she turned her back, the billy lowered his head and ran straight for Gna's behind. With one good butt, he sent her sprawling.

Trying to swallow her laughter, Bree choked. Instead, a giggle slipped out. Mikkel slapped his leg, echoing her glee. When Gna looked their way, both of them grew instantly quiet.

"Uh-oh," Mikkel said softly. "We've done it now."

"Is she the girl you're going to marry?" Bree whispered, suddenly curious.

When Mikkel didn't answer, Bree hurried forward,

offering her hand to Gna. "Can I help you up?" she said, her voice as sweet as honey in the comb.

But Gna shoved Bree's arm aside. Slowly, gracefully, Gna rose from the shore, brushed off her skirt, and whirled on Bree.

"I will *never* forget that!" Gna's eyes sparked her anger. "You are my enemy from this day forward. You will be my enemy forever!"

"Ah, Gna," Mikkel said. "Don't take yourself so seriously."

"Seriously? You aren't the one knocked to the ground by this—this—" Gna had no words for him. "This outlaw goat, that's what he is!"

As Gna stared after him, Bree's gaze followed hers. A short distance away, the billy goat had stopped. Looking at Gna, the goat seemed to roll his eyes. Then with all the dignity he could bring to the occasion, he started munching grass.

"Yes, he's an outlaw goat, all right," Mikkel answered in his most solemn voice. "I can see how dangerous he is."

As the billy set off again, the other goats followed. Zigzagging their way between the people on shore, they hurried toward green pasture near the longhouse.

"Where did they come from?" Bree asked.

"The out-farm—the summer pasture." Mikkel pointed across the fjord to where they had loaded the animals. "They've had good green grass all summer, but at the end of September we bring them down. If there was snow or ice on the mountain, we wouldn't be able to get them home."

Mikkel pointed to the steep side of a mountain farther along the fjord. "See that slanted line? There's a path for the animals to go up. That's where they come down when summer is over."

As Mikkel talked, sheep followed the goats. Then a cow, swinging her head from side to side, followed the sheep, still bawling her complaint. Bree looked after the cow and the billy now far up in the pasture. Remembering Gna, Bree giggled.

Gna whirled around. With one glimpse into her eyes, Bree knew. No doubt about it. Gna was her enemy.

Bree gritted her teeth. All her life people had treated her nicely. She didn't know how to handle someone like Gna. *But I'm going to learn. Somehow I'll get along with her. Maybe we'll even become friends.*

Then Bree remembered. Being a slave would no doubt set her apart from Gna.

With his sea chest on his shoulder, Mikkel started up the slope toward the longhouse and farm buildings. When he turned to speak to Bree, she sensed the change in him.

"Come," he said, his voice impatient now.

So, am I supposed to walk behind you? Bree almost flung out the words. The idea made her angry. More than once

Mikkel had told her his father was the mighty chieftain of the Aurland Fjord. More than once, Bree had wanted to spit back, "And I am a chieftain's daughter!" So far she had managed to hold her tongue.

Now she wondered about it. If her brother Devin managed to raise ransom money, what would happen?

Bree's thoughts scurried on. *If these terrible Vikings know I'm a chieftain's daughter, will they raise the price of letting me go? Will they demand so much that Dev can't pay what they ask?*

Ahead of Bree, Mikkel suddenly stopped.

TWO

MIKKEL'S SECRET

Mikkel swept his windblown blond hair out of his blue eyes. Turning, he looked back to the waters of the fjord. Strong and beautiful with sleek sides, his longship rested on the shore. As always, Mikkel's heart leaped with pride whenever he gazed upon his ship.

My Sea Bird. Always Mikkel had called it his. In his thinking, at least, it belonged to him. The Viking ship had served him well.

Tall for his age and with skin bronzed by the sun and wind, Mikkel felt like what he was—the master of a ship and leader of a crew of men. Soon after he turned fourteen, his father had put him in charge of this merchant ship that sailed from the Aurland Fjord to Ireland.

In Dublin, Mikkel had traded both skins and furs. Then he raided the Irish countryside, stealing precious gems and other treasures. Most valuable of all were the silver coins Mikkel had managed to collect.

Collect? Well, that wasn't quite the word. It wasn't what his father would call it, but for now Mikkel wouldn't worry about that. He was home. Gone were the dangerous moments on the open sea. Here he was, safe at last. He had even brought home valuable Irish prisoners. Soon he must face his father and some very big questions.

My *Sea Bird?* Deep inside where he didn't want to look, Mikkel wondered about it. Since his raid on the Irish monastery, he had asked himself what his father would do when he found out.

Turning to Bree, Mikkel saw the troubled look in her eyes. "Where do I go?" she asked.

"I'll show you." Along the shore were the other prisoners who had become slaves during Mikkel's raid on the monastery. *No matter!* he told himself. *They're only Irish. Plenty of other Vikings do what I did.*

Mikkel let a warm feeling of satisfaction fill his insides. This, the first voyage he led, had been successful in every way. He was coming home with his sea chest filled with treasure. Ignoring the shadow in Bree's eyes, Mikkel grinned just thinking about it.

But Bree did not smile back. Bowing her head, she stared at the ground.

She'll get over it, Mikkel told himself. *Before long, she'll like it here. She won't mind being a slave.*

Soon all the people in the mountains and valleys around the Aurland Fjord would know how well he had done on his first voyage. From this moment on, his fame would grow. In the great halls of the north his name would pass from one storyteller to the next. All the world would hear of Mikkel, son of Sigurd, mighty chieftain of Aurland!

But now Mikkel wondered where his father was. Busy, no doubt, seeing to the people under his care. Sigurd took his responsibilities as chieftain seriously.

Mikkel's chest swelled with the pride he always felt when he thought of his father. Then something else rushed in —a fear that Mikkel couldn't push aside as easily as the Irish prisoners. Deep in his heart Mikkel held a bigger secret, one he must keep from his father, no matter what the cost.

A moment later Mikkel saw him coming. With a strong step and long stride, Sigurd hurried from the river that emptied into the Aurland Fjord. On land owned by his family for generations, Mikkel set down his sea chest and faced him.

With gray-white hair and mustache and beard trimmed close to his face, Sigurd stood tall and straight. His powerfully built hands and shoulders still made Mikkel feel small, but he had learned to watch for the expression on his father's face.

Sigurd looked at him with gladness of heart.

Mikkel bowed his head in respect. "Father," he said.

Sigurd's smile was filled with the warmth Mikkel sought. "You are late," his father answered. "Did you have trouble?"

"A storm in the North Sea." When Mikkel told him about it, his father's eyes turned dark with concern. Three years before, Mikkel's older brother had been lost at sea.

Now Sigurd's smile showed his relief. Reaching out, he clapped Mikkel's shoulder. "It's good to have you home—to see you safe."

Then Sigurd glanced toward the fjord where prisoners still waited near the ship. "Who are these people who came in with you?"

"I have brought you slaves, Father."

Suddenly Sigurd's face held the stern look that Mikkel dreaded. "You have brought us people who need to eat, and winter will soon be upon us."

"I have brought you valuable workers."

"You have brought people who should be home with their families. I asked you to be a merchant. I supplied you with a ship, with men, and with goods to trade. Was it not enough?"

Mikkel's chin lifted. "From one raid I am a wealthy fourteen-year-old."

"But are you an honest fourteen-year-old?"

Deep inside, Mikkel felt the flush of anger move

26

from his chest up into his face. Again he bowed his head, but this time he wanted to hide his resentment.

As Sigurd turned, his gaze rested on Bree. "And who is this?"

Mikkel shrugged, as though it wasn't important. "A slave. An Irish lass gathered up from the countryside when my men raided a monastery."

Sigurd looked long and hard at Mikkel. "She is under my protection."

Mikkel lifted his head. "She is under my protection also. Bree rescued me from drowning and saved my life. I promised to watch out for her."

"See that you do," answered Sigurd.

When he extended his hand, Mikkel looked his father straight in the eye and shook on it.

"I need to welcome the others," Sigurd said. "We'll talk more at home."

As he watched Sigurd head down the slope, Mikkel thought again of the secret he must hide from his father. *If he finds out—*

Mikkel pushed away the thought. *He won't. My secret is safe. No one else knows. No one but me and one other person. And that person is far beyond the Irish Sea.*

Lifting his head, Mikkel grinned. *I'll get away with it. I'm sure of that.*

Now Mikkel wanted to set down his sea chest where

it would be safe. He'd find a place where he could look upon his treasure with no other eyes to watch.

"Pay no attention to my father," Mikkel told Bree as they watched Sigurd hurry toward the longship. "My father is a wise and just man. But no matter what he says, you're still a slave."

This time Mikkel watched Bree's face. A look as stiff as dried mud had slipped over her eyes and mouth. Mikkel knew what that meant. Sometimes Bree's mask slipped, and Mikkel saw how angry she felt. Other times she hid her feelings so he wouldn't know she was planning something. When Bree planned something, it was almost always escape.

Coming from the ship, Bree had walked behind him as a slave should. Yet even when she should feel like a slave, Bree somehow made him feel she was winning.

"You know," Mikkel warned, "if you try to run away, it's a very long trip across the mountains."

Bree waited, not looking at him.

"Any small boat you steal will not help you enough when the winter winds come."

Bree turned and looked back to the fjord, as though considering the idea.

"And there's no food or shelter along the way."

Suddenly Bree laughed. Even Mikkel saw the joke of it. Bree had already shown her ability to find her own food and shelter on a mountainside. And now when she smiled, it was as though the sun came out from behind the clouds.

Mikkel was almost fooled, but not quite. That smile of hers usually meant he had lost on every count.

Whatever she's planning, it's something big.

THREE

BIG BROTHER

The longhouse Bree had seen from the ship was strong and solid looking. The returning animals had already trampled the surrounding field. So far, no goats nibbled the grass on the roof.

"Everyone on the Aurland Fjord knows my father is a mighty chieftain," Mikkel said. "He is wise and just, but my father is much too strict."

Oh? Bree suspected she knew why.

"In the spring our assembly of freemen—our *ting*—will decide what to do about people who are lawbreakers," Mikkel told her. "But you will still be a slave."

"No, I won't."

"For as long as you live, nothing will change the fact that you're a slave."

As Mikkel walked on, Bree glared at his back. She wanted only to be home with her family again.

The farmhouse ahead was not unusually wide but very long. The long wall was built with a slight, outward curve that made the house wider in the middle than at the ends. It reminded Bree of the way a Viking ship was built.

When they reached the door, Mikkel stopped and looked around. "Home," he said, his voice filled with relief.

But Bree felt upset again. *Mikkel is home, but I am not.* As though she was really a slave, she reached forward and opened the door for him.

Mikkel stopped dead in his tracks. He waited as if he didn't trust her. It pleased Bree so much that she almost laughed in his face.

You think you'll win? she wanted to ask. She, Briana, best known as Bree, was an O'Toole. Anyone from the Wicklow Mountains knew that an O'Toole did not lose.

Looking Mikkel straight in the eye, she spoke. "No matter how often you tell me I am, I will *never* be a slave!"

Mikkel stalked into the house. Inside, Bree saw a large open room. Two rows of wooden posts held up the roof and divided the space. Near the center of the room was a long hearth with a fire pit surrounded by large flat stones. An iron kettle hung from a chain in the ceiling.

Mikkel's mother, Rika, was already there. Her face shone with the pleasure of having Mikkel home. Hurrying over, she again welcomed him. Then she caught sight of Bree.

At the look on Rika's face, Bree stepped back. If she had been able, she would have disappeared. But Rika was already asking, "Who is this?"

Mikkel grinned. "Your new slave, Mamma."

"My slave?" Rika was not pleased. "Where did this slave come from, and why is she here?"

"She's an Irish lass and my special gift to you," Mikkel said. "Bree is here to help you."

"Bree?" Clearly the name was not familiar to Rika.

"Briana."

"And why would I, your mother, need help with all the help I already have?"

Mikkel shrugged. "If you don't want it, Bree would be glad to go back to Ireland."

As he glanced her way, Bree straightened, filled with hope. "Yes, Mikkel, tell your mother that. I want to go back to Ireland."

Mikkel frowned at her.

Bree kept on. "I will be no help, no help at all. Such a strong woman as your mother—she needs no one!"

But now Rika was watching carefully, first her son, then Bree. "So—" Rika said slowly. "She speaks Norse?"

"Yes, Mamma." Mikkel smiled.

"And does she know anything about cooking?"

"No, no, I don't!" Bree lied. "I don't know anything!"

"Only how to make fish soup," Mikkel answered in his most serious voice.

"And, my son, does she sew?"

"No, no, of course not!" Bree lied again.

"Only when she is on a Viking ship and must make sealskin garments for herself and others."

"My son, can she take care of herself?"

Bree didn't even bother to speak. She only shook her head from side to side.

As though every muscle had slid out of Mikkel's face, he showed no expression at all. "Only if she is running away from Vikings and must survive on the side of a mountain."

"For how many days?" Rika asked.

"For six long days and six long nights."

"Ahhhh," Rika said. "No wonder you are late. I think this Bree would make a good slave, after all. Besides, when you are so kind as to bring your mother a gift—"

Mikkel bowed. "Yes, Mamma," he said softly. "I was only thinking about your well-being."

Thoroughly angry now, Bree straightened. "Mikkel, you will be sorry for this until the day you die! I will not be your mother's slave! I will not be anyone's slave!"

But just then a shadow crossed the open doorway. "Yes, you will," Sigurd said. "Our son brought you here.

You are under my protection. It is almost winter, and there is nowhere else for you to go."

"You see?" Mikkel exclaimed. "It's important to listen to my father."

"And to me," Rika said. "Come, Bree. I want you to show me how you make fish soup."

As she walked over to the fire, Bree did not look at Mikkel. Instead, she held her head high and her back straight. She was so angry with him that she was sure she could start a fire without a spark from any wood.

For Bree, making fish soup was easy. She had watched her mother from the time she was a little girl. Then, as she grew in her own cooking skills, her mam had always encouraged her.

Mikkel and his father sat down on a bench along the wall. Bree felt sure that at night those benches were used for beds.

While Bree worked near the fire, she listened to Mikkel and his father. But something bothered her. When Mikkel arrived with his ship, only a tear slid down his mother's cheek. Mikkel's father only clapped him on the shoulder. *If I came home, Daddy and even my brother Dev would kiss me on the cheek three times. Don't these Norwegians love each other?*

Instead Sigurd said, "Tell me again about your voyage."

When Mikkel talked about the storm in the North Sea, his father again showed his concern. Rika turned from the fire and walked over to the loom leaning against the wall. For as long as they talked about the voyage, she faced away.

"And what about your trading, Mikkel?" Sigurd said at last, and Rika turned back. "Did you use honest scales?"

Bree knew what that meant. A chieftain and farmer, her father was also a merchant. He often talked about the men who secretly added weights to their scales in order to cheat others.

"Honest scales? Of course, Father." Mikkel's answer came so fast, Bree wondered if it was really true.

Suddenly Bree felt glad for Sigurd and the honor with which he lived. Bree had no doubt that he led his people well. True, it would never be comfortable holding a guilty conscience before him. Bree had seen Mikkel's eyes when he thought he had gotten away with something. She had also seen his eyes when Mikkel knew that he hadn't.

He's hiding a secret from his father.

"Did you go to my friend Bjorn, the cobbler in Dublin?" Sigurd asked.

"Yes!" Mikkel seemed relieved to be able to say it. "He bought all the skins you sent him. Paid a good price too."

"And what did my friend Bjorn have to say about you, my son?"

"He sent you greetings, Father."

"And nothing more?" Sigurd searched Mikkel's face.

Mikkel flushed, then took a bag from within the larger bag of coins Bree had seen on the ship. It wasn't hard to tell that somewhere between here and the ship Mikkel had made two other bags of coins disappear. "And Bjorn sent trade goods—ready-to-wear shoes of the sizes you requested."

Sigurd nodded, took the coins, and weighed them in his hand. But his gaze never left Mikkel's face. "Why do I feel you aren't telling me everything?" Sigurd said at last.

Mikkel grinned. "I'm good trader, Father—a good merchant. That was the easiest part of the trip."

"No doubt. And the hardest part was the raid upon the people of Ireland?"

"One raid made me a wealthy fourteen-year-old," Mikkel said again, his eyes resentful.

"Tell me," Sigurd said. "How would you feel if it was your mother who was stolen away from her home?"

Mikkel glanced toward his mother. Again she turned away, this time picking up a piece of wood for the fire.

"I sent Hauk to teach you the ways of a sailor and a merchant. What was Hauk doing during this raid?"

"He was sick in Dublin—so sick he almost died. We couldn't start back until he felt better—"

"So when Hauk was not looking, you and the other mice played as you wished?"

Mikkel looked away, not answering.

Sigurd's eyes were stormy now, a look as angry as the North Sea. "Did you kill anyone?"

"No." Mikkel said.

"Did your men?"

"I don't know."

"You don't know, or you don't want to know?" Sigurd asked, as Hauk had done.

Mikkel looked down. Here and there pieces of straw lay on the hard earthen floor, and Mikkel pushed them with his boot.

Leaning forward, elbows on his knees, Sigurd covered his face with his hands. Without moving, Rika stood at the fire, waiting and watching. When at last Sigurd looked up, he seemed to have aged ten years.

"My son, if you had stolen from someone in our country, I would expect you to pay back what you stole. I would expect you to pay something more to restore honor. But how can I ask you to go back to the place where you stole so much? How can you ever pay enough for taking people from their families?"

Sigurd sighed, as though barely able to speak. "Unless you find a way to set your actions right, you'll be a slave to what you have done."

Mikkel looked up. "Me? I'm not a slave." Clearly the idea startled him. "I'm a free man, just like you."

"No!" Sigurd said. "You're a slave to whatever you serve."

Mikkel looked away.

"My son," Sigurd went on. "Find a way to set right the wrong you have done."

Still standing near the fire, Bree forgot to stir the soup. In one thing Mikkel was right. Sigurd was a wise and just man. Bree felt grateful for the truth that he spoke. But Bree also felt sure of something else.

There's still something Mikkel is trying to hide. What secret grips him with terror when he thinks his father will find out?

One thought kept going around in her mind. *When I learn Mikkel's secret, I'll hold it over him. I'll use it as a way to get home.*

During the voyage here, Bree had learned that Norwegians ate two meals a day—a day meal in the early morning and a night meal in the early evening. When the family gathered for their evening meal, Bree saw Mikkel's grandparents for the first time.

Grandmother was small and frail with white hair that waved softly around her face.

Grandfather looked much like his son, Sigurd. Both had the same mustache and powerful hands. But now Bree guessed that Grandfather's health kept him from doing all that he'd like.

Rika set long, narrow tables close to the benches along the wall. Still showing Bree where everything was, Rika pointed out the wooden spoons, then put bowls close to the large pot hanging over the fire. From a loaf of bread that was still slightly warm, Bree began cutting slices.

Mikkel's fifteen-year-old brother, Cort, came in just as everyone was ready to start eating. Instead of Mikkel's light blond hair, Cort's was a darker blond. Though they looked very different, both had blue eyes and stood like proud young warriors.

Sitting down on the benches along the wall, the two began talking as if only a day had passed since they had last been together. "So," Cort asked, "how did you like seeing the world?"

Mikkel's quick look took in his brother's face. "Only half the world," he said, as if it wasn't important.

"Nothing exciting happened? No captives taken?"

For an instant Mikkel's gaze rested on Bree. Just as quickly he looked away, but not before Bree saw the resentment in Mikkel's eyes.

"No great wealth to bring home?" Cort's voice sounded rock-hard, like a hammer slamming against stone. As Bree watched, a cold look settled across Mikkel's face. *So they don't like each other,* she thought. *I wonder why?*

Then she remembered. It was Mikkel's oldest brother, Ivar, who had died at sea. Ivar was supposed to inherit the land. "My favorite brother," Mikkel had called him. So this Cort was *not* his favorite. And by right of inheritance, he would own the land if Sigurd died.

Taking up a ladle, Bree dipped it into the large kettle. The first helping of fish soup was big, and she set it before Mikkel's grandfather. Next she served Grandmother and set a larger bowl in front of Sigurd. When she served Mikkel's mother, Rika, she set the bowl down carefully, trying to show her the honor she would give her own mother. Rika glanced up and smiled her approval.

But when Bree served Cort a larger portion, he pushed it aside. "More," he commanded.

Bree picked up his bowl. As she started back to the fire, Cort stretched out his foot. Suddenly Bree tripped.

FOUR

HAYLOFT HIDEAWAY

As Bree caught herself, soup spilled over Mikkel's shoulder. Jumping to his feet, he ripped off his shirt before the liquid burned him.

Sigurd glared at Cort. "We will have no more of that."

A half smile filled Cort's face. "Sorry, little brother. Welcome home."

Bree caught the look between the brothers. Then she saw the pieces of fish clinging to Mikkel's shirt. Left there, they would begin to smell.

Beneath the surface of everything Cort did, Bree felt an anger he did not bother to hide. A spark of resentment seemed to enter his eyes whenever he looked at Mikkel. *Why would an older brother resent one who was younger?*

Mikkel seemed to accept his brother's welcome. But when he sat down again, Mikkel had a flushed look that told Bree he was trying to control his anger. Secretly she felt glad that someone seemed to be getting the better of Mikkel.

Bree returned Cort's bowl with a larger portion. As she started back to the fire, Mikkel opened his mouth, as though planning to speak. Bree had no doubt that if he did, his anger would pour out in a torrent. But suddenly Mikkel looked toward his mother.

A half smile on her lips, Rika waited as Mikkel turned to look at his father. Tipping his head in respect, Mikkel spoke. "It's good to be home again."

As Bree swallowed her laughter, she choked. Quickly she moved away from the family, but there was something she now knew. At sea she had seen Mikkel as a bold leader who seldom showed fear. No wonder he knew how to be a tyrant on board the Viking ship! He had learned those traits by being picked on by an older brother.

When Bree returned with a bowl for Mikkel, she stayed as far as possible from Cort's feet. She gave Mikkel the biggest portion of all.

Glancing up, he grinned at her, as though saying, "I'm starved all right. Thank you." Dipping his spoon into his bowl, he ate as though famished.

When Bree finished serving, she took her own bowl to the end of the room. Away from the family, she sat down on a bench along the wall. From there she could see the fire and the line of smoke rising to the hole in the ceiling. For the first time since being taken captive, Bree felt glad she was a slave. She wouldn't have to sit with the two brothers.

But then Bree felt lonesome for her own family. If her fourteen-year-old brother, Dev, had reached home, his words would spill out, making a story of everything. Mam and Daddy, Adam, Cara, and Jen would all lean forward, not wanting to miss a word. *And I'm not there.*

In her whole life Bree had never felt so alone. Then she remembered Keely. *I have to believe I'll find her. I have to believe there is some good reason for my coming here.*

In this strange land, the thought of her sister offered hope. *But what if I fail? We'll never see our family again.*

When tears slid down her cheeks, Bree straightened and promised herself, *That is not going to happen!*

As she brushed away her tears, Bree glanced back to the fire. Mikkel's mother was watching her.

By the time Bree finished eating, she had decided on a plan. She would start by making friends with the dogs on the farm. When she went outside, wooden bowl in hand, she knew they expected someone else.

"Here, kitty, kitty, kitty," she called, and soon the cats were there. She gave them a small part of the leftover scraps, then waited.

One by one, the farm dogs came near. At first they

eyed her with the look all dogs give a stranger. Bree waited again, letting them get used to her. Then she scraped another small amount of fish leavings into a bowl.

The biggest dogs leaped forward, eating with greedy appetites. A short distance away, a mid-sized black dog sat down on his haunches. Tipping his head from side to side, he studied Bree with bright, beady eyes. As though welcoming her, he woofed.

Bree went to him at once and gave him the rest of the scraps. "I will call you Shadow," she told the dog. "And we will be friends."

When Bree finished cleaning up the dishes, Rika selected a key from the ring on her belt. Going to a chest, she opened it and handed Bree a wool blanket. As she felt its thickness and warmth, Bree understood the gift Rika had given her. Running her hand over the cloth, Bree smiled her gratitude. "Thank you."

But then Bree wondered about it. *A blanket from the family supply? Why?*

Picking up an oil lamp, Rika carried it with her. A narrow passageway led from the large open family area past smaller rooms to a door into the barn. As Bree entered the stable, she felt at home at once.

It was dark there, but from the day she was born, Bree had lived on a farm in Ireland. For as long as she could remember, she had known green fields and cows that bawled their displeasure when a dog nipped at their heels.

She remembered the sheep and the lambs following close after their mothers.

Warm with the crowding of animals, filled with the scent of hay, their barn had always been a comfort to Bree. Reaching out, she smoothed the neck of a cow that looked her way.

Rika turned, saw Bree stroking the cow. "You like animals then? I do, too. They are good friends."

Rika explained. "Sometimes you will work here—" she stretched out her hand. "And sometimes with me. We have servants who help with the rest of the animals and outside work."

"Servants?" Bree asked.

"The children whose parents don't have enough food for them in our long winters. The old people who are not strong enough to work a long day. And some people who are strong and work well."

"Servants," Bree said again. Suddenly her next words spilled out. "But I am a slave?"

"Yes." A strange look passed through Rika's eyes, then was gone. But the tone of Rika's voice was final, allowing no more questions.

A slave. Unable to look at Rika, Bree glanced away. She didn't want to think about being a slave. But then she wondered how many would share the stable. "Where are the servants?"

"We have other buildings for them. During the day,

some of them work here. Some help me. And some work outside."

As Bree looked around, Rika spoke again. "Make a place for yourself," she said. "In the cold, dark months of winter the animals help keep the stable and house warm."

Bree nodded. The warmth given off by the animals took the chill from the air. Yet Bree had no doubt in her mind. An Irish winter in the Wicklow Mountains could not be compared to a Norwegian winter. She would burrow deep beneath the hay.

In that large dark barn with no windows, Rika allowed just one light—a small oil lamp that could be set in only one place—on a wooden shelf safely away from any hay. Whatever Bree did, it must always be put out whenever she went to bed.

"In the night I want you to care for Grandmother," Rika said.

Bree stared at her. "But I will be here. And she will be in the house with you."

"In the room closest to the fire," Rika said. "When she calls in the night, I will expect you to answer. Give her comfort."

"Comfort? But how will I hear? A closed door—the door to the house—will separate us."

"You will hear," Rika said. "You will hear."

When Mikkel's mother left, Bree picked up the oil

lamp and started down an aisle between stalls. *Is that a horse I'm seeing?*

Drawing close, Bree held up the light. *Yes! Not one horse, but two.* As Bree drew close, one of the horses turned and looked at Bree with large beautiful eyes.

"Tomorrow when the sun is up, I'll open the door so I can really see you," Bree promised the mare.

Still holding the warm blanket Rika had given her, Bree studied the location of the stalls, the animals, and the door to the outside. Bree felt pleased. By using that door, she could come and go during the night without the family knowing.

I'll look for Keely, Bree promised herself again. *And when I find her, we'll escape over the mountains, or through a fjord, or—*

Bree's imagination knew no bounds. Whatever it took, they would find the way back to Ireland. *How can we fail if we're together?*

But take care of Grandmother? Bree was used to sleeping soundly. In spite of what Rika said, how would she possibly hear through a closed door?

Then Bree saw what she needed. Near the door into the house, a wooden ladder led upward. In the loft above was a large open space filled with hay.

When she climbed to the loft, Bree found the hay fresh and sweet smelling. Breathing deep, she imagined long grasses growing on the mountainsides. Norwegians dried their hay on the slopes. Someone must have carried this hay home in his boat.

Bree smiled. Gathering her blanket around her, she burrowed down in the hay. Soft and comfortable it was. A warm hideaway. Just right for an end-of-September night. *If it's safe here, this will suit me well.*

In the next moment she was asleep. When Bree woke, it was to the sound of moaning.

FIVE

SECRET MESSAGE

At first Bree thought it was the wind under the eaves. But the sound increased and had a strange human quality. What was it? And why did the moaning make her afraid?

Listening, Bree tried to figure out what it was. The sound was louder now and grew louder all the time. It seemed to come from inside the house. And then Bree knew.

Pushing aside her blanket, she felt her way down the ladder. In the dark aisle between stalls, she stumbled against posts. At last Bree found her way to the door into the house. Rika met her there.

"Come," she said. "I'll show you what to do."

Mikkel's mother led Bree down the hall to Grand-mother's room. Beyond lay the large area where the rest of the family slept on benches around the fire. The door of Grandmother's room and places along the wall were open to the heat. As Bree drew close, the moaning was loud enough to fill the entire house.

Two small oil lamps flickered in the air currents, and shadows danced up and down on the ceiling. Bree found Grandmother lying on a wide bench built into the wall. A soft pad protected her old bones from the hard wood, but her discomfort went far beyond that. Grandmother had flung one blanket to her feet and another across the room. Her moans had changed to loud wails.

Bree stared at her. This was the quiet, fragile woman she had met at the evening meal?

Rika went to her and knelt on the earthen floor next to the bench. With her arms around Grandmother, she spoke. "Grandmother, wake up! This is Rika! I'm here to comfort you. Wake up!"

But Grandmother flung her arms against Rika. "Step aside! Get away! She comes to take me! Get away, get away!"

Rika patted her back. "It's a dream, Grandmother."

"No! Such a strange looking woman. Why does she come for me?"

Rika sighed. "Our gods will take care of you—"

"But she is a goddess—" Grandmother was fully awake

now, but her eyes still held their fear. "Take care, Rika! I don't want her to hurt you!"

"She won't!" Rika exclaimed. "I'm strong. That's what my name means. I'll defend you against her."

Grandmother shook her head. "No one is strong enough to defend me against this one!"

"I've brought Bree," Rika said. "She'll stand with me, defending you against the goddess. Bree will be sure that you're well cared for."

Turning, Rika motioned to Bree. "Come close," she whispered. "Let Grandmother hear your voice."

But Bree stood there, rooted to the dirt floor. Grandmother's fear frightened her.

"Come," Rika said again. "Speak to her."

When Rika drew her forward, Bree had no choice. As she knelt down next to Rika, her hands were shaking. What could she possibly say to help the old woman? Just seeing the fear in Grandmother made Bree want to turn and run.

"Speak," Rika commanded. "Let her get used to your voice."

Close to Grandmother, Bree saw the whiteness of her face. How could a nightmare be that terrible? But then, out of her deep wish to help, Bree began to speak.

"I am a new friend," she said softly.

"No, no! No new friends!" Grandmother cried out. "I

don't trust anyone new—The goddess comes from the fog
—the rising mists—"

"Grandmother, this is Bree," Rika said. "Remember, she served you fish soup at supper?"

Again Rika motioned. "Speak to her," she whispered. "Let her hear the softness of your voice."

"I come from a far land where the mists settle between the mountains," Bree said.

"No, no! No mists, no far land!"

Rika sighed. "Don't talk about Ireland," she whispered. "Whatever Grandmother sees, it must be the same as your country."

Ireland the same as something fearful? Bree felt angry now. But somehow she had to set that aside, or she'd be here all night.

"Grandmother," she said. "I am Bree. You can trust me."

Trust. The word seemed to fill the air between them. In the dim light of the two small lamps, Bree could see that Grandmother was listening.

"I will take care of you," Bree said. "Listen to a song I learned when I was just a young girl."

When Bree started to hum a lullaby, she felt afraid again. Hadn't her brother Dev often said that her singing was fit only for the cows? And usually Dev spoke truth. But the minute Grandmother closed her eyes, she moaned again. It was easier for Bree to hum than to think of what to say.

Then Grandmother stretched out her hand. Taking it, Bree held it between both of hers. Rika drew up a blanket, recovered the one thrown across the room, and tucked it around the older woman.

The words, Bree thought. *I can't remember the words of the lullaby.* But then she knew it didn't matter. Grandmother wouldn't understand the Irish anyway.

For a long time Bree knelt there, humming and whispering kindness to the woman who was so afraid. When Rika slipped away, Bree felt sure she had gone back to bed.

At last Grandmother's hand relaxed. The frightened lines in her face disappeared. When she started breathing evenly, Bree knew Grandmother was asleep.

Withdrawing her hand, Bree tiptoed out. When she reached the door into the stable, she slipped through and climbed the ladder. Sinking deep into the mound of hay she had claimed for her bed, Bree pulled the warm wool blanket around her.

Tired as she was, Bree could not go back to sleep. Instead she lay there thinking. *Is that why I got a family blanket? So I wouldn't bring fleas to Grandmother?*

Whatever the reason, Bree felt grateful for the warmth of the soft wool covering her shoulders. But she couldn't get beyond one thought. *What is there in this strange land that would make a kind old woman so afraid?*

55

In the early morning the family had their day meal while it was still dark. This time Bree cooked porridge, a warm cereal made in the large pot hanging over the fire. Again Mikkel and his father talked. Cort leaned back against the wall, seeming to listen, but not taking part.

"I grieve for you, my son," Sigurd told Mikkel. "I wish you had walked the path of an honest and wise merchant. I would have given you the *Sea Bird.* Now you must show me that you can be a merchant, not just a raider."

"I'll do better next time. I'll prove to you—"

Sigurd shook his head. "Not next time. At the end of three trips we'll decide whether the ship is yours."

Resentment flashed through Mikkel's eyes, then was gone. "I'll make you proud, Father," he said.

Sigurd's gaze met Mikkel's. "You've told me that before."

"This time I mean it. On my next trip I'll take two ships."

"Two?"

Mikkel's face showed his excitement. "I have it all figured out. I'll take the *Sea Bird* with men and trade goods the way I did this summer. And before we leave I'll build another ship."

"With what?" Sigurd's question shot out like an arrow. "How do you plan to pay for this ship of yours?"

"With my share of the money. And the silver coins I collected."

"The coins you collected where?"

"From the Glendalough monastery. And the people."

Sigurd's face looked like a thundercloud. "Mikkel—"

"I know, I know. If I borrowed money—"

"Borrowed?"

Mikkel changed the word. "If I took money from a man living on the Aurland Fjord, it's an offense punished by death."

Sigurd nodded.

"But if I repaid the money—and if I paid the man something extra to say I was sorry I dishonored him—"

"The *ting,* our assembly of freemen, might outlaw you. Or they might let you stay."

"Yes." Mikkel smiled, as though he had thought it all out. "But if I collect something—"

"Take something." Sigurd's voice was as hard as the rock walls of the mountain at the edge of the farm. "*Steal* is the word."

But Mikkel didn't seem to hear. "Today I'll begin work on the ship," he said quickly. "I'll get men together. I'll ask a master shipbuilder—"

"No!" Sigurd's cry echoed his pain. "You aren't hearing me! No, no, no!"

"No?"

"You will *not* get your men together. You will *not* ask

a master shipbuilder to help you. I, your father, am a master shipbuilder! You will *not* ask someone else."

His eyes watchful, Mikkel waited.

"I trusted Hauk to teach you, but you took advantage of his poor health. You did things your own way. No more."

"No more?" Mikkel asked. "No second chance?"

"You will not take advantage of me the way you did Hauk. From now on I will go with you."

"We'll work together?"

To Bree's surprise, a grin lit Mikkel's face. *He really loves his father!*

"We'll work together." Sigurd stretched out his hand. When Mikkel shook it, both of them looked happy about the agreement.

But Bree looked toward Rika. With careful movements Mikkel's mother set down the large bowl in her hands. "So now," she said softly, "I not only have one ship on the open seas, I have two."

The moment she could, Bree slipped out to the barn. As the light of day reached between the mountains, she opened the door near the horses. It was as she thought. Both the mare and gelding were a pale reddish color. But then Bree stood back, staring.

Their thick light-colored manes stood up, making their unusual coloring even more noticeable. A dark stripe ran through the mane, down the center of the back into the tail. Seeing it, Bree felt awed by the beauty of the horses.

"I will call you Flurry," she said as she ran her hand along the powerful neck of the mare. "When the wind blows cold and snow flurries come, I will warm my heart with thoughts of you. And we will be friends."

A short time later, Bree saw Mikkel and his father working down near the fjord. Soon a crew of men gathered around a long narrow building.

"What are they doing?" Bree asked Rika.

"Repairing a shed. They'll use it as a boathouse to build another ship." Clearly Rika was not happy about the project. But then she gave Bree good news. "Soon they'll go upriver to cut down trees. They'll do as much as they can before winter."

Bree could hardly hide her excitement. *If Mikkel and his father are gone—*

Then Bree remembered Cort. More than once she had caught the spark of resentment that entered his eyes whenever he looked at Mikkel. Bree could never forget that Cort might stretch out his boot to trip her. Even if the others left, she must watch out for him.

Tonight I'll start looking for Keely, Bree promised herself. *If I find her, we'll plan how to escape when the men leave.*

Later that day Rika sent Bree to the river for water. Bree blinked as she stepped into the sunlight. After the dim light of the house, she felt glad to be away from the oil lamps, the fire, and the smoke that drifted toward the ceiling. Whenever she was indoors too long, Bree felt like the prisoner that she was.

Now blue waters lay a short distance away. The afternoon sun lit the waterfall spilling over the mountain on the other side of the fjord. The river that emptied into the fjord flowed through a valley. A small cluster of houses lay between Sigurd's farm and the river.

When Bree reached the river, she found a large flat stone where she could kneel and dip water out of the stream. In a cluster of trees away from the houses, she discovered a tucked-away hollow between boulders. Setting her buckets down, Bree looked around, then slipped into the shelter from the wind. There she sat down and sorted out her thoughts.

First she wondered about Lil. She and the eight-year-old girl had become friends on the trip from Ireland. In the days they were together, Lil had put away her scared feelings and found the courage to win.

Then Bree thought about her sister Keely. *She has to be close by. How can I find her?*

And Devin. Countless times Bree had wondered if her brother reached home safely. *If Dev was here, what would he tell me?*

Bree knew at once. "Courage to win," he would say. "Jesus our Lord is Savior and King."

When they were very young it had started as a way to

encourage one another. If Bree crossed her arms over her chest, Devin knew she was praying for him, though he faced the biggest bully in the Wicklow Mountains. It became a signal that helped them when they needed it most.

But now Bree's loneliness overwhelmed her. It was much easier to have courage when she and Dev were together. If courage was doing the right thing even when she was afraid, how could she possibly win?

Yesterday she had lied three times. In the middle of Grandmother's nightmare, she had lost all courage. God seemed far away—not even real.

Then Bree remembered something she had needed to learn a long time ago. *If I ask God to help me in whatever I face, He will give me the courage to win.*

Tucked down between the boulders, Bree found a warm spot and started to pray. "Please, Lord. Please help me. I can't do this."

In that moment she sensed a small voice from deep within. *You can't do it? But I can.*

Bree smiled. Sometimes she forgot how simple God made things. *I can't do this. But God can.* Hugging the thought to herself, Bree repeated it over and over again.

Already Bree felt better; and she knew what she needed. "Lord, in this strange land where I can't even talk with friends like Lil, will You be my Friend? My invisible, always-with-me Friend?"

As Bree started back to the house, she crossed a soft stretch of ground near the river. Suddenly she stopped.

Close to the water, someone had drawn a face—a round face with two dots for the nose and a single line for a curved-up mouth. The two eyes had that same curved-up line, as though they were smiling. Two long lines with X's showed a braid, and on top of the face was a funny-looking tuft of hair.

As Bree stared at the drawing, she started laughing. The braid had to be Keely's, and the tuft on the top of her head clinched it. When she was a baby, it was all the hair she had!

Keely! It was you I saw! It really was you!

Dropping her buckets, Bree knelt down, and traced the tuft of hair with her finger. Then she kissed the face. It was the closest she could come to kissing her sister.

Leaning back on her heels, Bree looked around, searching the boulders along the river, the nearby pines, and then the mountaintops. Nowhere did Bree catch a movement. Nowhere did she catch even a glimpse of someone half hidden from sight.

Bree felt both excited and disappointed. *Keely, I know it's you. But, please, will you show me where you are?*

SIX

GNA!

Then Bree realized she had no idea how long the drawing had been there. Had Keely come during the night or early morning? Bree had no way of knowing.

Again, she stared at the soft ground. *It has to be Keely,* Bree told herself. *She wants me to know she's here. But why won't she let me talk to her, hug her, tell her how glad I am to see her?* That's what Bree longed for with all her heart.

As Bree watched, the water lapped closer, reaching out for the face drawn in the sand. *I almost missed it,* Bree thought. *I almost missed it, but I didn't!*

When she returned to the house, Mikkel's mother said, "You're late."

"I'm sorry," Bree answered but would say no more.

"Do you know how to weave?" Rika asked her.

"Of course!" Bree said, her voice stiff. "When I was just a young girl, my mother taught me. That's how we do it in Ireland."

But the upright loom that leaned against the wall of the longhouse was different from the loom Bree used at home. Rika set her to work tying long vertical threads called a warp on the upper part of the loom. At the bottom of each thread, Bree fastened a weight to hold the thread tight during weaving.

As Bree brought the shuttle on a horizontal line, going back and forth between the vertical threads, she held dreams in her hand. Dreams of finding Keely after six long years of being apart. Dreams of talking and laughing together. For hadn't Keely drawn a happy face with the mouth turned up in a smile?

After the evening meal, Bree again took food to the dogs. Whenever there were even a few left-over scraps, she made sure that she was the one giving them.

This time the dog Bree had named Shadow tipped his head from side to side, as though looking her over. When he came forward, he wagged his tail.

"Good dog," Bree said. Kneeling down, she scratched behind his ears. Shadow wiggled with delight. Even his curled-up tail looked pleased. From that time on, he followed Bree around whenever she was outside.

The moment she could, Bree went out to the stable. By

the light of the oil lamp she pulled together everything she needed. The night would be crisp and clear, and she wanted to use every hour while the moon was full. But first she must wait long enough for the family to fall asleep. Then she would quietly open the stable door and slip outside.

Each night I'll go a different direction, Bree promised herself. *I'll find the farms and houses close by. Maybe I'll even find Keely tonight.* If they talked together now, they could escape when Mikkel and his father were gone.

After blowing out the lamp, Bree climbed the ladder. As she sank deep into the hay, she listened. Outside a wind had come up. Alone in the dark stable, Bree heard it under the eaves. Then she heard the creaking of timbers and wondered if someone walked where she could not see.

Courage to win, she told herself and wished her brother was there. *Courage to win, Bree*, she thought, reminding herself of all the ways her family lived that courage.

Twice she nearly fell asleep, and then at last she decided it was time to leave. Down the ladder she went, through the aisle between the stalls. She had lifted the latch on the door leading outside when she heard it.

The moaning started soft and low, and built like the mountains along the fjord. *Grandmother!*

Bree dropped the latch, and leaped away from the outside door. Pulling off her cloak, she dropped it behind a mound of hay. When Rika opened the door from the house, Bree was nearly there.

The next morning Rika told Bree that later that day she could have a few hours off for a religious festival. Everyone would meet in a sacred grove of trees high above the fjord.

All day long, Bree wondered what she would find there. Would it be like her own family going to church? Or would it be something she didn't know or understand?

Shortly before sunset, the family set out with Sigurd, Rika, and Grandfather leading the way. Except for Grandmother, who stayed home, the rest of the family trailed behind them. Then came the servants, and last of all, Bree.

At the river they took boats across to the other side, then walked up a steep hill. When they reached a grove of trees, there were several bonfires around a grassy area. The people who had gathered together faced an open area with a flat stone and some statues. From the greatest to the least, everyone seemed to have their expected place. As a slave, Bree stood near the back.

To her surprise it was Hauk who led the festival. Bree had first seen him on the voyage from Ireland. With gray-white hair and a flowing beard, he was the person Sigurd had trusted to teach Mikkel to be the master of a Viking ship.

Now Hauk's piercing eyes looked out from beneath bushy eyebrows. The flickering bonfires brought shadows to his face and the hollows of his cheeks.

Bree shivered. She had hoped to find the peace she felt in her church at home. Instead, she remembered Hauk on the Viking voyage. During the worst of a storm, she had seen him crawl over to his sea chest, reach inside, and hold onto the holy book stolen from the monastery.

The people Hauk led seemed to believe in the power of their gods to help them. But did Hauk? Bree only knew there was no mistaking the shadows in his eyes.

As Hauk stepped back, a girl in a gold dress stood in the open area. Her long blonde hair fell to her waist. Around her, the flames of the fires rose in the darkness.

Gna! Bree barely breathed the word, but a nearby woman turned to shush her. Bree hadn't seen Gna since the day Mikkel's ship came into Aurland. By now Bree felt more sympathetic about how she would feel if knocked over by a goat. *If I weren't a slave, would we be friends?*

Then Gna started to sing. Bree had always wanted to be a singer, but long ago her brother had made things plain to her. Again Bree remembered it was best that she sing to the cows. And it did seem to help. Their Irish cows were good milkers. But Gna—

Bree wanted to catch every word. At first she had trouble with the Norse words she didn't know. Then Gna's clear voice reached into the farthest corners of the open area. People caught the excitement, stomped their feet, and raised their hammers to Thor.

Bree missed going to church with her family. She

wanted something to fill the empty spaces in her heart. Instead, what Rika called a festival was filled with a heavy, cold darkness. As Bree listened to Gna's words, something inside her started to change.

At first Bree thought the cold was just from being outdoors. Then she realized it was a spiritual coldness unlike anything she had ever known. When Bree felt uneasy, the jiggly feeling she had inside told her that something was wrong.

"What is it, Lord?" Bree started to pray. "What do You want me to know?"

In the next moment, Bree sensed the still small voice that she recognized. A quiet message prompted her from deep inside. Sometimes that quiet message brought comfort on the darkest night, but now Bree sensed a warning. *Leave.*

Leave? Bree asked, her eyes wide open as she prayed.

Leave.

Bree didn't wait. This was the voice she knew. The voice she had heard since a young child. The prompting she sensed when she asked God for help or heard the Bible read.

Quietly, with the stealthy movements she had learned since becoming a slave, Bree edged away. Step by slow step, she moved into whatever space she could find between people.

As Bree reached the last row, she glanced back. Gna was watching.

She knows I'm leaving, Bree thought. *She'll remember.*

Bree waited for a few minutes—but Gna waited too. Though she kept singing, she watched Bree. Finally Bree stepped behind a tall man, waited again, and then backed away.

As Bree started down the side of the mountain, she wondered what to do. She couldn't take a rowboat. If she did, it would be on the wrong side of the river for the family going home. Finally Bree sat down on a large rock.

On the mountain above her, the flames of the closest bonfires spilled into the darkness. With every breath she drew, Bree felt relieved, as though she had escaped something strange and terrible she didn't understand. What was it she had known as people lifted their hammers to Thor?

From long ago came words she had memorized from the book of John, never guessing she would be a slave. "You will know the truth, and the truth will set you free."

Truth.

Then she *did* understand. The real slaves were the people locked in the darkness of their gods.

Yes! That's what bothered her. And with it she knew something else. It fell upon her like a flash of light in a dark and stormy night.

Lord, whether I am slave or free, I belong to You. And You have set me free!

Deep within Bree an idea began to form. If she was going to find Keely, she needed freedom to roam. But now Bree felt sure that God also wanted her to do something more.

SEVEN

BROWN ROBE

By the time Mikkel found Bree, others were waiting to use the boats. But Mikkel felt upset about having to search for her. "Why did you leave?" he asked, his voice filled with anger.

Bree jumped up from the rock where she was sitting. "I wanted to pray to the God that I know."

Mikkel laughed. "We're pleasing the gods *we* know. And we're praying for the last ship out."

Bree glanced down the river to the fjord. "It's very late, isn't it?"

As Mikkel stood there, a snowflake drifted down, but he still expected an answer.

"Why don't you worship our gods? You aren't in

Ireland anymore. It would help you to worship the gods of this land."

"My God is everywhere," Bree said. "He knows I'm here."

"How can anyone, even a god, be everywhere? I have many gods and call on the ones I need."

Bree's clear gaze met his. "I don't want to come here again."

Mikkel stared at her. "Why? You get out of work if you come."

On the hill above them, the bonfires still flickered and burned. Mikkel saw more snowflakes against the light of the flames. Faster and faster they swirled around the river.

But Bree seemed to not notice. "Mikkel, I'm not a slave. I don't think like one. I can't act like one. I need to be outside—to climb the mountains the way I did in Ireland."

"No!" Mikkel would not risk having her run away. His crew of men would think he was weak if she succeeded again.

"I want something more to do," Bree said. "Something where I help other people."

Though Mikkel had never considered the idea, it wasn't foreign to him. For some strange reason, it was what his mother and father did.

"You help Grandmother," he said.

"It's not making any difference. Aren't you tired of

having Grandmother wake you up every night? I could read stories to her from the book you stole from the monastery."

Inside, Mikkel felt sparks of anger again. "The book the man in the brown robe gave me as a reward for being careful of his people."

"Brother Cronan said that?"

Mikkel nodded. "He said he'd make a trade. A book of great value for the lives of his people."

"A trade," Bree said softly. "Then you gave the book to Hauk. Is he going to tear it apart to keep the gems?"

Mikkel shrugged. "You'll have to ask him. I told him what Brown Robe said—"

"Not Brown Robe—Brother Cronan. He was my teacher at the monastery school."

"When Brown Robe handed the book to me, he said, 'I will pray that this book is well used.'"

Bree smiled as though she had received a secret message. It made Mikkel curious.

"Then Brown Robe said something even stranger. He said, 'The person who reads this book will receive God's sovereign protection from you Viking raiders.' What's sovereign protection?"

For a moment Bree wondered what to say. Would Mikkel think he could do anything he wanted and God would make it right?

"It's like the protection a king or queen gives," she

finally said. "But God can protect people wherever they are. He's promised to be with me always."

Mikkel's laugh mocked her. "Your God promises to be with you always?" But then Mikkel thought again. *I could use more protection when I go to sea. I better make sure that Bree is along.*

In that instant Mikkel made up his mind. "I'm tired of having Grandmother wake me up every night. You say there are stories in the big book? Maybe since my grandparents are very old—"

"Yes!" Bree exclaimed. "They'd like to hear the stories. That is, I'll tell them stories if your mother lets me walk outside."

"Outside in winter? Do you know what you're asking? Besides, I can't trust you."

"Unless I give you my word."

Mikkel wasn't fooled by the meek look in Bree's face. "And you will give me your word?"

The hard sound was back in his voice. Bree must have no doubt that she would remain a slave. A slave who could do only what he allowed her to do.

EIGHT

THE TALKING COW

When Bree heard the hard sound in Mikkel's voice, she knew she needed to get his permission at once. "If I give my word, I'll keep it," she said.

Mikkel's angry gaze met hers. "I know you will. That's why I ask."

As though she were lining up soldiers one against another, Bree thought about it. If she gave her word that she wouldn't run away, she couldn't escape across the mountains. If she found Keely, they would be held here by her own promise. But if she *didn't* give her word, she had no way to search for Keely. She had tried and couldn't get beyond Sigurd's farm.

Though Bree wanted a trade, this was more than she bargained for.

Mikkel grinned. "It's a hard choice, isn't it? I can see your thoughts march across your face."

I hope not. Bree felt the hot flush of embarrassment rise in her cheeks. Aloud she said, "I doubt it."

Mikkel's grin faded. The hard look returned to his eyes. "I can at that. So, Irish lass, you better make your choice now and be glad if I give you even one small drop of what you call freedom."

For only a moment longer, she waited. "I promise to not run away." She raised her chin. "Not without telling you."

"No conditions," Mikkel shot back. "You promise to not run away."

Bree clenched her fists. She was giving up her freedom for Keely's sake. But Bree felt her sister needed freedom even more than she did.

When Bree spoke, her voice sounded as hard as Mikkel's. "In exchange for not running away, you will give me two things. Ask your mother to let me tell the stories in the big book. Ask that when I finish my work, I can walk in the mountains."

Mikkel searched her face, as though making sure she spoke truth. For an instant he glanced down at her clenched fists. Then he nodded.

Bree lifted her head. The snow flurries had stopped.

High above her, the bonfires were dying down, but she saw them as a symbol of all she did not want. Turning her back on them, Bree unclenched her fists and stretched out her fingers.

On the walk back to the longhouse, she prayed with her eyes open. *Lord, whether I am slave or free, I want to serve You. Not because I must, but because I love You.*

As Mikkel and his father left the next morning, Bree and Rika stood outside the longhouse. Bree asked Rika about the ship that was still out.

"It's a merchant ship with many men," Rika told her. "It left months ago filled with trade goods. The master of the ship is a man we all love. Most of the men on board are from fjords and mountains close by. It was this way three years ago—"

When Rika did not go on, Bree knew that she couldn't. Bree also thought that she knew the rest of the story. "Was it three years ago when your oldest son sailed away and didn't return?" she asked softly.

Rika's face was set, her lips pressed together, as if she could not speak.

"Ivar?" Bree asked. "His name was Ivar?"

Rika nodded. Though her face seemed carved in stone, her eyes showed her pain.

Soon Mikkel, Sigurd, and their crew of men disappeared around a bend in the river. Rika said they were going upstream where trees grew on the slopes. "They'll sleep in the closest barn or find hunting shelters in the mountains."

"Shelters?" Bree asked.

"Small huts built under a rock overhang. They have stone walls and a place to see out. High in the mountains, men have dug deep narrow pits. When they hunt reindeer, they hide the pits with branches. When the wind blows cold—"

Rika didn't need to finish. Already Bree had felt the wind coming down the fjord, and it was only October. But from now on Bree would watch the mountaintops. Maybe she would see a reindeer running free. A reindeer that did not fall into a pit.

When they went inside, Bree discovered that Mikkel's word was good. A package wrapped round and round with sealskin lay on a table. When Rika took off the layers, she held up a book with a white calfskin cover. Firelight caught the sparkle of the precious gems on the cover.

Rika gasped. Brought to the monastery by pilgrims from many lands, the gems had great value. Hand-copied by Brother Cronan, a monk at the Glendalough Monastery, the book contained the four Gospels.

Rika traced her hands over the cover, lightly touching each jewel. "What do we do with it?" she asked.

"I want to help Grandmother sleep."

Rika rolled her eyeballs. "That's impossible! Her nightmares go on and on."

I know, Bree thought. *For me too. And I want to search for Keely!*

A slow smile crept into Rika's face. "Well, I guess neither of us has anything to lose."

Later that morning, Bree and the grandparents sat down on one of the benches close to the fire. Even in the dark room the light of the flames caught the precious gems on the calfskin cover.

Like Rika, Grandmother reached out and lightly touched each gemstone. But then she sat back and waited, as though knowing the real treasure lay inside.

Bree carefully opened the pages. Turning the book for Grandmother and Grandfather to see, Bree pointed out the bright colors and beautiful designs in the hand-drawn letters. To Bree it seemed that light shone from the pages.

Again Grandmother reached out. With a careful touch, she traced a beautifully drawn letter and nodded. Once more she sat back, as though waiting.

As Bree looked down at the Latin words, she felt like giving up before she started. *How can I possibly read a language I'm still trying to learn?*

She also needed to translate the words into the Norse language. Bree didn't know whether the trade language she had learned from her father used all the same words as the people on the Aurland Fjord. But then as she asked God for help, He showed her what to do. Brother Cronan had taught her well, so she could read enough of the words to remember the stories. She could explain the stories in her own words or through promises she had memorized.

Bree decided to start with a thought that meant especially much to her right then. "This book tells us about truth," Bree said. "Jesus said, 'You will know the truth, and the truth will set you free.'"

At first Bree found it easiest to not look up from the big book. Then she sensed a quiet movement.

As Bree talked, Mikkel's grandmother straightened up. Her shoulders back, she sat erect and strong but had a faraway look in her eyes.

Is she even hearing what I say? Bree wondered. It was a relief to see Grandmother sitting quietly instead of moaning in her sleep. But Grandfather stared at Bree so intently that she shivered. *What is he thinking? Am I doing something wrong?*

That afternoon, Bree and Rika began weaving the sail for the ship Mikkel would build. Eventually the many long strips they wove would be sewn together to make the gigantic sail that sent a Viking ship running before the wind.

On some days women helped Rika with her work. On other days she worked alone. Bree was starting to understand the meaning of the keys on Rika's belt. They seemed to be a symbol of all she must do to manage the farm when the men of the family were at sea.

As Bree worked, she kept thinking about Mikkel and his father. How long would they be gone?

After her first few nights in the house, Bree had decided on a plan. She would wait until Grandmother woke up, help her settle down, and then creep out to search for Keely. But Bree soon learned she could never guess when Grandmother would have a nightmare. And if she wasn't there when needed, Rika would know at once.

Mikkel had been right. His mother needed help with her work. It surprised Bree that Mikkel had been concerned enough to notice. It showed a kindness in him that Bree didn't expect.

But now, after reading comforting words from the big book, Bree felt more hopeful. Hadn't Grandmother been helped by her reading? Tonight she would surely sleep better.

Instead, Grandmother woke up crying again. As one night after another fell away, Bree grew more and more desperate. *How long will this keep on?*

Soon Mikkel and his father would be back. Without doubt they would stay in Aurland for the winter. When the snows of winter were upon them, how could she possibly search for Keely?

As Bree lay awake at night, she felt the barn grow colder. Alone in the stable, she heard the meow of the cats and the quiet movements of the cows. Other times she heard the wind in the eaves and the creak of timbers. And still other times Bree wondered if she heard footsteps outside the barn.

Sometimes a dog gave sharp warning and started other dogs barking. Always Bree listened. Would she hear the click of the latch if someone opened the outside door?

Working hard all day, awake much of the night, Bree finally was exhausted. Lying on her bed of hay, she stared up at a roof she could not see and decided she had been a slave long enough.

"I can't stand this, Lord," she prayed. "I promised to serve You, but don't You love me? Don't You care what happens to me?"

In the dark stable, the horses stamped their hooves.

"I hate what I have become!" she whispered in her anger. "I'm starting to think like a slave. I'm starting to think I cannot change what is happening to me!"

Knowing that made her afraid. "How can I have the courage to win when I hate every part of my life?"

Bree pushed back her blanket. "I don't want to be a slave," she declared without realizing she spoke aloud. From the darkness below, a cow mooed.

"I hate being a slave!"

Again the cow mooed.

"What's more, I will *not* be a slave!"

For the third time the cow mooed. Bree sat up. "Be quiet!" she ordered. "I'm talking to myself, and you're interrupting."

In the silence that followed, Bree felt relieved. *Good!* she thought. *Someone around here is listening to me!*

But then she spoke aloud again. "I hate my life. I hate it, hate it, hate it! I'm always serving, serving, serving! No one ever says I'm doing a good job. No one ever says thanks. They just ask for work, work, work!"

"Mooooooooo!" The longest one yet.

Suddenly Bree laughed. Throwing aside her blanket, she climbed down the ladder and started toward the shelf where she kept the lamp. When she remembered she had no way to light it, Bree headed for the cow instead.

Bree stumbled around in the darkness. When she found the right stall, the cow turned her way. Bree felt the movement with her hands and stroked the cow's neck.

"I will call you Molly," Bree told her. "And we too will be friends."

And then, standing there in the darkness, Bree sensed the small inner voice she knew well. Like a nudge it came, as though she knew words without hearing them with her ears.

How can you be a light if there is no darkness?

"Ohhh!" Bree exclaimed. "You remembered! Being

here—being a slave—isn't just a terrible mistake? Something that happened because You looked the other way?"

Though the barn was so dark that Bree could not even see her own hand, she felt like she was bathed in light.

NINE

DAUGHTER OF THE KING

Starting the very next morning, Bree was the one who milked the cow she called Molly. It didn't matter that other people milked the rest of the cows. Bree always milked Molly. And Bree always sang to her, for that was the time when Bree talked to God.

I am a chieftain's daughter, she told both Him and herself. With that proud knowledge, Bree lifted her head.

No, she decided. *I'm more than that. I am the daughter of a King—the King who created the heavens, and the earth, and the entire world, including this cold, dark land of the North!*

Yet there was something Bree was learning. She could feel good about herself when everything went right. When she had family, friends, and neighbors who loved her. But she didn't have those people anymore. *So what do I do, God? What do I become?*

In the quiet of the stable, Bree waited. And then, as she milked Molly, Bree knew. *I become a person who respects myself. Not because everything is going right. But because I know how God sees me.*

When Bree went outside, a dusting of snow lay on top of the mountains. Along the fjord, the brown leaves of an apple tree rustled in the wind. As Bree dipped water from the river, she clutched her cloak around her but still felt cold.

Today there was a thin layer of ice on the fjord. Now, as often before, a young woman came to the river, but looked downstream at the fjord. An older woman did the same. People always turned toward the direction where ships sailed in from the sea.

Some of the people glanced that way quickly, as if pretending they hadn't looked. Some walked down to the fjord and stared into the blue depths that now looked black with cold. And some stood on the shore, as though unable to do anything else.

Seeing them, Bree knew that they waited. As she watched them, Bree wondered about her brother Devin. *Where is he? Did he get home safely? Has he managed to collect ransom money and begin the trip here?*

Then, as always, she asked herself, *Can Dev possibly come before winter?*

Later that day Mikkel, his father, and the other men returned from upriver. While still in the forest, they had begun hewing the wood to the size and shape they needed.

Many of them carried long slender pieces of wood for overlapping planks in the sides of the ship. Others brought heavy pieces for braces or supports. Still others carried the trunk of a very tall tree on their shoulders. Bree felt sure that was the mast, the center pole that supported the sail.

Last of all came Mikkel with the part of a tree where a branch meets the trunk on his shoulder. Naturally strong at the bend, it would become the steering oar of the ship. Because the men used freshly felled timber, it was easier to shape than weathered wood.

Watching them, Bree felt surprised by all that Mikkel and the men had already done. True, Sigurd had helped them. But if Bree was honest she had to admit that Mikkel was a born leader.

The next morning he hurried through the meal. It was easy to see that Mikkel and Sigurd were eager to be at their work. They wanted to use every day before the winds of winter made it more difficult.

When Bree took a warm cap to Grandfather, she found him with Mikkel.

On the flat ground inside the boathouse the men had started by laying a keel on wooden supports. Next they bolted stem and stern posts in place. The ship had a double-ended hull with both the bow and the stern built the same way.

Mikkel's grin was wide, his face glowing. While aboard the longship he called *Sea Bird*, Mikkel had shown his love of sailing. Other times he talked about seeing far-away places and distant lands and seas. Now this ship would be his even more certainly than the *Sea Bird*.

"Where will you go?" Bree asked him when he stopped working for a moment.

Mikkel shrugged. "Wherever I wish. When the wind blows fair I'll be gone."

Bree felt a knot in her stomach. *Not to Ireland, I hope.*

When Bree was in the barn with the animals, she felt her happiness return. Wouldn't her brother Dev one day come to rescue her?

When no one could hear, Bree sang to the cow she secretly called Molly. Of a certainty, Molly must have had relatives in Ireland. Whenever Bree sang in the Irish, Molly would turn her head, looking back at the girl who milked her. After one long moo, the cow faced forward, tending to business again. But her milk streamed into the pail as though she liked Bree's company.

And the chickens! As the nights grew longer, Bree knew the chickens should stop laying eggs. How could it be that with fewer hours of sunlight, they still dropped their eggs into any mound of hay? Often Bree had to search out the eggs to find them before they froze. Whenever she brought them to Mikkel's mother, Rika showed her surprise.

But Bree loved the horses best of all. Such horses were fit for a king. Running her hands over their backs, Bree stroked their necks and whispered into their ears.

By now, the horses recognized her step and greeted her whenever she entered the stable. As Bree brushed the coats that were thick from the cold weather, she ran her hand over their cream colored manes with the dark stripe. Both horses felt like new friends.

At the same time, Bree grew more and more anxious about the winter that would soon be upon them. Though Bree put in a long day's work, Rika sometimes let her go into the mountains. Then one afternoon she said, "My good friend has a birthday. I want you to bring her a gift."

Carefully Rika wrapped towels around six precious eggs. Carefully she nestled the eggs in a basket with a stout carrying handle. And then to Bree's great delight Rika told her to cross the river and follow the path upstream.

"But take care," she said. "The way is steep and dangerous. You Irish are used to walking in the mountains?"

Bree smiled. "When I was just a young girl—"

"Oh, yes, of course!" Rika said. "You Irish!"

It had become a joke between them, for Bree too

often said, "That's the way we do it in Ireland." Finally Rika drew back, saying, "I will hear no more about all the things the Irish can do." But now she smiled.

Carrying the basket of eggs, Bree set out. The dog Bree secretly called Shadow followed close behind.

Wherever she walked, Bree watched for landmarks— ways she could find her direction if she came that way at night. The promise between her and Mikkel stood, but if she were ever released from that promise, Bree wanted to have a plan.

The farm where Rika's friend lived was nestled in a hollow of the mountains. When Bree drew close, dogs and children ran to meet her. When Bree gave Rika's gift to the woman who lived there, her face shone with gratitude.

"For my birthday?" she asked. "From my friend Rika? Tell her thanks and thanks and thanks again."

That was the day Bree found her Irish friend Lil. When Bree went back outside, Lil followed her to the beginning of the trail. After they hugged each other, Bree stood back, looking at the eight-year-old who had become a close friend on the voyage here.

"How are you doing?" Bree asked like an older sister to a younger.

"I miss my family," Lil told her. "But every time I do, I ask God to fill me with His love. And He does." When Lil smiled, it was as though a light shone behind her eyes.

As the woman of the house looked out the door, Lil

spoke quickly. "Bree, remember how you told me about your sister Keely? Does she have hair the color of reddish sand? Blue eyes? Freckles across her nose?"

"A long braid and a funny tuft of hair at the top of her head?" Bree asked.

"I've seen an Irish girl like that," Lil said. "But I don't know where she lives."

Then Lil grinned. "You know, I still need to get you back to Ireland. My cousin Tully wants to marry you when you grow up."

Marry me.

All the way home, Bree clutched the thought to herself. On the day Mikkel raided the Irish countryside, her secret dreams for the future had been stolen away. For as long as Bree could remember, Tully had been a friend to both her and Dev.

When Bree returned from upriver, she hurried around the back of the barn. Walking alongside the mountain at the edge of the farm, Bree came to the shore of the fjord. Near the boathouse were small trees that hid Bree from view of the house.

Talk of Tully made her lonesome for home. In all this time she still had no idea where to find Keely. And now, Bree had to face something more.

Whenever Bree saw people waiting for the last ship, her hope died just a bit. How could Dev possibly come this late in the season? Worse still, what if he was on a ship that was lost at sea?

Then as Bree prayed for the last ship out, she realized something. Wise and good Sigurd reminded her of her own father, a respected Irish chieftain. Kind Rika reminded her of what it meant to be under the care of her own mother. But Mikkel?

Mikkel wrecked my life! He destroyed my dreams!

Whenever Bree thought of him, she felt a knot of hurt deep inside. Leaning forward, Bree buried her head in her lap and began to sob.

Then in the midst of her sobs, Bree remembered. God had set her free. But her hurt and resentment for what Mikkel had done was so great that she was not willing to set him free. For what seemed like the one-hundredth time, she prayed, forgiving Mikkel. This time she even asked God to bless him.

Instantly Bree wondered why she had ever prayed that. She almost took her prayer back. She could only feel glad that Mikkel wasn't there to hear.

TEN

LOST FOREVER?

As Mikkel came out of the boathouse, he caught a glimpse of Bree as she tucked herself down behind trees farther along the fjord. Mikkel stopped, watched, and waited. *Is Bree hiding until she can slip off over the mountains?*

Suddenly Mikkel didn't want Bree to go. The thought surprised him. *I don't want to have to search again,* he told himself. Yet Mikkel knew it was more. He worried about Bree's safety.

Then from the other side of the trees, he heard sobs. Soft at first, as if she didn't want anyone to hear. Then the heart wrenching sobs of someone who could no longer hold back the pain she felt.

In that moment Mikkel suddenly wished that Bree would leave his life forever. Listening to the sobs that seemed to tear her apart, Mikkel knew the truth of his father's words. *You're a slave to whatever you serve.* In that terrible moment of truth, Mikkel despised himself.

How can I possibly set things right? He couldn't go back to Ireland, not to the Wicklow Mountains where Bree lived. The angry Irishmen would kill him for ruining their lives. *And Bree's father?* Mikkel shuddered just thinking about him.

Even if I returned Bree safely, her father has every reason to hate me. Her mother—Bree's mother will hate me even more. All these months of having Bree gone from their family—

For the first time, what he had done seemed real to Mikkel. Until now he had been able to push it aside. No longer. Bree's angry looks at him, her open hatred for what he had done, had never touched him like this. Bree's sobs changed all that. They even changed the way he saw his own mother and father.

Now, as he watched his mother, father, and all the townspeople wait for the Viking ship to return, Mikkel remembered the day the word came about Ivar. *Lost—gone forever.* Only now did Mikkel understand that it was the same in any language, any land. People loved their own and always would. By leading a Viking raid, he had torn those families apart.

Bree's sobs were quieter now. *She'll get over it,* Mikkel

tried to tell himself. Yet he had to face the truth. Maybe someday Bree would learn to live here, but she would never get over losing her home. She would never be totally free of that ache Mikkel himself knew. The lonely ache that came each time he remembered that Ivar was gone forever.

As Mikkel stepped back inside the boathouse, he again wished that Bree would slip away over the mountains. Just disappear from his life. But then, strangely enough, he didn't want that either.

ELEVEN

DEV'S SURPRISE

Still wiping tears from her face, Bree came out from the trees near the fjord. As she started along the sheer rock wall of the mountain, she looked down. Someone had placed small stones on the slanted side of a large boulder.

Bree stared at the patterns. One was a straight stick with upper and lower arms. The second pattern was a torch. Another secret message? Bree felt sure that it was.

Keely? Could it possibly be? As Bree wondered what the message meant, Mikkel spoke from behind her.

Bree jumped. Whirling around, she faced him with a sinking heart. *What if the message gives Keely away?*

With one swift movement Bree stepped between the

small stones and Mikkel. But he was studying her face, and Bree wondered if he could tell she had been crying. Instead of saying something, he moved around Bree and looked down at the boulder. "What's this?"

Bree shrugged. "I don't know."

"Interesting," he said. "This has to be a torch." Mikkel traced his finger around the flame. "Maybe someone wants to meet at night. But this?"

Mikkel pointed to the stick with two arms. "It's not one of our runic symbols."

Trying to pretend it wasn't important to her, Bree stood back, but her thoughts raced ahead. *If it's not a runic symbol, it must be the letter K.*

Just wondering about the possibilities, Bree felt as if she could leap over the highest mountain. Then she remembered. She must hold that secret to herself. She could not let her excitement show in her face. But Mikkel had given her a key as important as the keys Rika carried on her belt.

As Mikkel headed for the boathouse, Bree was thinking back. *When my sister Keely was taken by Vikings, how old was she? Six? Seven?*

One thing was certain. Keely hadn't learned to read and write as Bree and Devin had. *Does Keely know that in the Irish her name starts with the letter K?*

Possibly. Bree could only guess. But the more she thought about it, the more hopeful she felt.

Late that afternoon when it was time to read to the grandparents, Hauk came to the door. Bree took one look at him and swallowed hard. When Bree first saw Hauk on the Viking voyage she had been afraid of him. Then as the *Sea Bird* crossed the dangerous North Sea, Bree had glimpsed him in a different light.

But now Hauk had come. Ready to argue? Or to hear for himself?

As they sat on benches near the fire, Bree looked from one to the other and wondered what to do. Grandfather helped her out. "Tell Hauk about this man Jesus."

Bree started by telling about His birth. "Our God loves us so much that He sent His only Son as a baby. Because there was no room in an inn, He was born in a stable. His mother laid Him in a manger—a feeding trough—a long narrow box that holds food for animals."

Grandmother smiled. A pleased look filled her eyes. But Grandfather's unblinking stare made Bree uncomfortable. The sharp look in his eyes seemed to go right through her. Whenever Bree explained something, he listened as though testing every word.

Hauk asked even more questions than Grandfather. Bree did her best to answer, but she could never tell what Hauk was thinking. Before long, he made her so nervous that Bree stumbled over her words. Finally she stopped talking.

But Hauk motioned to her. "Go on, go on. Why is your God so loving?"

The next time Bree looked up she caught the hint of a smile in Grandfather's eyes.

Bree couldn't figure out what was happening. Then she saw the look in Grandmother's eyes. It started the same way—almost as if someone had turned on a light.

As the grandparents glanced at each other, Bree wondered, *Did I say something strange? Did I use a word the wrong way?* She didn't think so. But the grandparents certainly knew something she didn't.

The next day when Hauk came in, he paused in the open doorway. In spite of the cold, he stood there for a few minutes, staring at the fjord. Later, after Bree read for a time, Hauk stood up and walked back to the door.

Closing the big book, Bree watched him. Again Hauk gazed at the long narrow strip of water that led between steep mountains to the sea. "Soon the fjord will freeze over," he said.

Turning, Hauk came back. "Please. I don't know how to pray the way you do. Will you pray to your God for the ship that is late?"

When Bree went for water the next morning, the wind carried snow on its breath. During the night, ice had formed in the fjord, and now the thin clear sheets lay in heaps on the shore. Hurling its way across the open, the wind stirred up waves and left white flecks of foam.

Though it was early in the morning, people stood on both sides of the river that emptied into the fjord. Today not just slaves or servants were there to carry water. Today landowners waited and watched. Women with a chain of keys at their waist stood quietly. Children stopped their play to look at the fjord.

All of them, young or old, gazed in the direction where the long, narrow waterway led to the sea.

Then, soft on the wind, Bree heard it—so soft that at first she thought she imagined it. Moments later the sound of music drew closer. Lively trills filled the fjord, pushing aside the cold and the fear.

Panpipes? The small wind instrument that Bree loved?

The high clear notes echoed against the mountains and leaped into Bree's heart. *Pipes?* she wondered again. *Pipes on a Norwegian fjord? Could it possibly be?*

Pipes belonged to Ireland. Pipes belonged to—

Then Bree heard it. The sweet clear notes of an Irish lullaby. Then Bree knew.

Dropping her buckets of water, Bree caught up her skirt and raced along the river to the fjord. A moment later a Viking ship rounded the bend in the rock walls of the waterway.

By the time Bree reached the edge of the fjord, whoever was playing the pipes had stopped. But Bree had no problem spotting her brother. Always Bree had been sure that he would be the one to rescue her. As the Viking ship drew close to shore, Devin stood at the bow.

As though a wave of the sea surged forward, people surrounded the ship, calling shouts of welcome. Near at hand, a young woman held up a child. When a man on board waved to him, the boy leaned forward, wanting to be held.

Moments later, the ramp went out. One Viking sailor after another picked up his sea chest, balanced it on his shoulder, and hurried off the ship. And then, carrying only a cloth bag filled with all he owned, Devin stood in front of Bree.

Like their father, Devin had the black hair and deep blue eyes of the dark Irish. Now his eyes seemed lit with excitement. And his laugh? Dev was so glad to find her that his laugh tumbled out of him.

Looking at him, Bree forgot everything else. "Dev! I can't believe it's you!"

Reaching out, Devin gave her a warm brotherly hug, then kissed her cheeks three times. When he stood back, he took Bree's hands and looked her in the eye.

"Are you all right?" he asked.

"Now that you're here, I'm perfect." As Bree opened her arms, he gave her another hug. Bree was so over-whelmed that she began weeping.

Clearly embarrassed, Devin patted her back. "There, little Bree, everything is all right now." Not since she was very young had he called her that. At the sound of it, Bree stopped crying, as she always had.

Devin reached into the bag he had set on the ground. Bree took one look at the handkerchief he held out and backed away. Even at a glance, Bree knew she wanted no part of blowing her nose in it.

Devin laughed and Bree laughed with him. Never in her life had she been so happy to see someone.

But there was something new about her brother. In the time since Bree had seen him, he seemed to have grown taller. *Is that it?* Bree wondered, and then she realized it was something else.

The hardship that had fallen on the family because of Mikkel's raid had aged Devin. But was it more?

"Mam? Daddy?" Suddenly Bree felt afraid for them.

"Except for missing you and Keely, they're fine. Mam says that when she prays she has peace about you."

Peace. Her mother actually had peace when she knew almost nothing about what happened to her? And then Bree remembered something. God had given her peace, too. Strange. How did both of them know peace in spite of all that had happened?

"Adam?" Bree asked about her seven-year-old brother.

"He took care of Cara and Jen until Daddy got to the hiding place and took all of them home."

Filled with relief, Bree smiled. "And that awful day when the Vikings came. What was it you told Adam?

"That if he could care for two little girls, he could be an Irish chieftain."

Bree's laughter filled the crisp air. "Oh, Dev, it's so good to see you!"

"And I have another surprise." Devin leaned forward to whisper in her ear. "Don't say a word. I have ransom money."

Ransom money? Bree drew back, checked his eyes to be sure her brother wasn't teasing. She felt sure that rescuing her from Mikkel's clutches would take a good deal of money. How could Dev possibly have collected that much money already?

But her brother put a finger across his lips, as though saying *shush!* Whatever questions Bree had, they would have to wait. Already Devin was looking around.

When he found the man who appeared to be the leader of the Viking crew, Devin led Bree over. "This is Ingmar, the man who gave me safe passage from Ireland. He's a trusted friend of a shoemaker in Dublin. Bjorn the cobbler said I would be safe with him."

When Bree looked up into Ingmar's face, she felt stunned by the look she saw there. This was no young man who chose to go a-viking because he wanted to raid the Irish countryside. The kindness in Ingmar's eyes reminded her of Sigurd.

"Ingmar, my sister Bree," Devin said. "So quickly I

have found her! I cannot thank you enough for giving me safe passage here."

Ingmar grinned. "And when the wind blows fair, I'll take both of you to Dublin. You'll be free again."

"Free?" Bree hardly dared breathe. "I will be free again?" Just thinking about having this kind man take them home seemed so overwhelming that Bree felt weak. Then as she saw Mikkel taking long strides their way, she felt angry.

"So! Who do we have here?" Mikkel asked, looking at Devin.

"My passenger," Ingmar answered.

"*Your* passenger?" Mikkel scoffed. He shook his head. "You're wrong there!"

"I promised him safe journey to the Aurland Fjord."

Instinctively Devin stepped over, next to Ingmar. He pulled Bree alongside.

"Then you gave a promise you cannot keep. Devin is my prisoner."

"*Your* prisoner?"

"*My* prisoner. My men took him captive during the raid at Glendalough."

Ingmar turned to Devin. "Is that true? You didn't tell me."

"But Mikkel set him free," Bree said quickly. "Mikkel even said to him, 'Go, while you have the chance.'"

"And you went?" Ingmar asked.

A still, cold look had settled over Devin's face. Seeing it, Bree felt afraid. "Dev raced up the hillside," she said quickly. "Mikkel watched him go."

"Is that true?" Ingmar demanded of Mikkel.

"In a weak moment—"

Bree remembered the moment clearly. How could she ever forget? She had asked Mikkel, "How many graves do you have in your family cemetery?" In that instant Bree had known something had shattered Mikkel's life. Seeing the expression on his face, she had pressed for Devin's freedom. And Dev won.

But Mikkel no longer appeared upset by the death of his brother. His face was cold and hard, his eyes angry and unwilling to give. "So, you brought ransom money for Bree?"

Devin met his gaze, but his eyes held no answer for Mikkel.

Mikkel's scoffing laugh broke the silence. "Of course, you brought ransom money for Bree. Why else would you come?"

Still Devin held his gaze. His blue eyes looked long and hard at Mikkel. But Bree could not see beyond the thoughtful look in her brother's face.

She had seen that look before—a look of firm purpose to meet whatever Mikkel decided to do. But Bree also knew something else—that behind that unflinching gaze, those blue eyes that would not give way—Devin was praying. In that moment Bree remembered.

With two quick steps, Bree moved from Devin's side to where her brother could see her without looking from Mikkel. In the next moment Bree crossed her arms in the signal she and Devin had used since they were children. "Courage to win, Dev," Bree was saying without words. "Jesus gives us the courage to win."

For one instant Devin's eyes flicked her way. When Devin also crossed his arms across his chest, it looked as though he had taken a battle stand.

Mikkel looked from Devin to Ingmar. "He was my prisoner. He is my prisoner again."

"No!" Ingmar declared. "You set him free. He remains free. When the wind blows fair, I'll take both of them back to Ireland."

By now the crowd that gathered seemed to have drawn a line in the sand. On one side stood Ingmar and the men coming off his ship. On the other side were men from Mikkel's ship. Devin stood in the middle of that line.

"So!" Mikkel told him. "You *do* have ransom money. Even Ingmar is not foolish enough to think I would let Bree go without it."

Reaching out, Mikkel grabbed Devin's bag, and began opening it. But Devin was angry now. As he snatched the bag from Mikkel, it split, and a bag of coins fell out.

Before Devin could catch it, Mikkel grabbed the bag and held it high.

"Mine!" he declared.

"Mine!" Devin answered, reaching for it. But Mikkel swung around and held the bag behind his back. His men drew close as if protecting him.

As their angry mutters grew, Bree heard their words. "The boy is our prisoner all right. We took him captive. Why should he go free?"

Bree clenched her hands. The frightened emptiness in her stomach changed to a knot of fear that told her something even worse was coming.

Behind Ingmar, his men were muttering, too. Without doubt they had grown to like Devin on the voyage here. But if it came to a bag filled with coins, where would they stand?

"The money is not yours!" Ingmar said to Mikkel. "Nor is it Devin's. He brought a ransom to set Bree free."

Mikkel glared at him. With one swift movement he pulled his sword from his belt. "I know how to settle this!"

TWELVE

BREE'S BIGGEST FEAR

Ingmar shook his head. "We are blood cousins, Mikkel. We will not let a question of money destroy our family."

"Go," Ingmar said to the man who stood behind him. "Get Sigurd. Our chieftain will settle this matter."

"No!" declared Mikkel, as though knowing what his father would say. "The *ting* will settle this matter."

"But that doesn't meet until spring."

Mikkel's hard laugh seemed to echo along the waters of the fjord. "Until then Devin can rot in jail. And I will hold the ransom money."

"No!" With long strides Sigurd reached the people standing on shore. The authority Bree had often heard in his voice was even stronger now.

"Who is this?" Sigurd asked, looking at Devin.

"Bree's brother, Devin," Mikkel answered, his voice angry but respectful.

"I promised him safe passage," Ingmar said quickly.

"He brings ransom?" Sigurd asked.

Ingmar nodded.

As Sigurd looked from Ingmar to Mikkel, Bree knew that Sigurd would allow no argument.

"I will hold the ransom money," he declared. "No one will take even one coin from this bag. When spring comes upon the land and our *ting* meets again, we will decide. We will hear each freeman who wants to speak. And when we cast our vote, we will decide whether a person who brings ransom can become a captive himself."

His body stiff and straight with anger, Mikkel stepped back, but Bree felt afraid. First for her brother Devin, then for what Mikkel might do. Bree also saw the anger in Ingmar's eyes. He had given a promise, and the promise had been taken from him.

"Now—" Sigurd looked first at Ingmar, then at Mikkel. "Both of you go with Devin. Take him to the jail. Tell the jailer I have ordered his safekeeping."

Reaching out, Mikkel twisted Devin's arm behind his back. Watching Mikkel, Bree felt angry again. Then she felt sick. But when she tried to follow Devin, Mikkel, and Ingmar, Sigurd stopped her. "Go to the house," he said.

When Sigurd entered the longhouse that evening,

Bree hurried to the door. She bowed her head in respect, but her voice was strong when she spoke. "Why did you put my brother in jail? You know he's done nothing wrong."

"I put him there for safekeeping," Sigurd answered. "His own safety."

"And Mikkel's." Bree was determined to bring the real problem out in the open.

But Sigurd met her honestly. "And Mikkel's. I will do what I can so that blood does not flow in our family."

In that moment, Sigurd suddenly seemed old. But his steady blue eyes held a look that Bree knew from her own father. No one would change Sigurd's mind.

When Bree visited Devin the first time, she found the jail easily because she heard him playing the pipes. A set of pipes bound together, the wind instrument was straight across the top and slanted from a shorter to a longer side at the bottom.

"Why was your ship so late?" Bree asked Devin.

"Storms," he said.

"Storms? Not one? Many?"

"In the North Sea."

"What did you do?" she asked.

"Pray like I've never prayed for anything in my life. Except when I prayed for you, that is."

Bree knew what that was like. Mikkel's ship had also met a storm in the North Sea. But then Bree looked around. The jail cell in which Devin lived was small and dark, lit only by one oil lamp. Part way below ground, it was also damp and so cold that Bree shivered even with her cloak on.

"It's dirty here," she said. Dirt she could see in spite of the poor light.

Devin shrugged as though it wasn't important.

"Ask the jailer for a pail of water. I'll scrub it myself."

"No," Devin said. "I'll scrub it after you're gone."

Bree held her nose. "It stinks. It's a hole in the ground. It's cold. It's dark."

"It's all that. Please, Bree. Just sit down." Devin offered her a wobbly three-legged stool, but it was better than the dirt floor on which he sat. His legs crossed, he made himself comfortable and said, "I just want to look at you. I want to believe you're really here."

Bree smiled. She too could not stop looking at her brother. "I didn't know if I'd ever see you again," she whispered.

"I still can't believe I found you."

"Now that you're here—now that I know that Mam and Daddy, Adam, Cara, and Jen are all safe—" Bree broke off.

Again she realized that Dev had changed since she last saw him. It was as though he had grown used to looking far across the sea. Had the pain of separation from her and the rest of the family given him that long steady look?

Then this brother who always watched out for her asked her, "Bree, how are *you* doing?"

His question brought tears to her eyes, and his hug warmed her heart. "Courage to win, Dev," she said when she could speak again.

"Courage to win, Bree. Jesus our Lord is Savior and King."

For a moment longer he looked at her, then cleared his throat. "Bree—the ransom money—"

Already Bree had started to hate that money. What if the Vikings didn't give it back? What if she had to stay here forever?

"Even the very poorest people in the Wicklow Mountains gave something. People traded honey, or sheep, or anything they had so they could set you free."

"Free," Bree said. The word seemed to echo between them.

"Free." Devin's answer bounced against the stone walls, flung itself around the room.

"Free." Bree's biggest fear was that she would never be free again. That the Vikings would leave her brother to rot in jail, never to see the light of day. That Keely would never be returned to their family. And then Bree remembered.

"I believe I've seen Keely," she said.

The next morning when Mikkel left to work on his ship, Bree followed him outside. He was still angry with her, and she with him. After all he had done to Devin, Bree wanted to never look upon Mikkel's face again. But there was something she needed to know.

"According to your religion," she began, "what happens when you die?"

Mikkel didn't like the question, she could tell. But then he said, "I'll go to *Valhalla*, a large hall where heroic warriors go. A young maiden will come and take me there to feast and to fight."

"But you're not a heroic warrior."

"Not yet," Mikkel admitted. "But I will be by the time I die."

As always, Bree hated his prideful look. "What makes you so sure?"

Mikkel grinned. "What makes you think I won't be?"

Bree had no answer for that, but she still didn't know what would help her with Grandmother. "What about people who are sick or old like your Grandmother?"

"There's a different place for her." Mikkel's voice sounded careless, as though it didn't matter since it wasn't his final destination. "It's twilight there—half day and half night. It's a cold place with freezing fog."

"Is it a place where you would want to go?" Bree asked.

"Even Mamma says she doesn't want to go there."

"And your father? Where will he go?"

"To a place where wise and just leaders go."

"Wouldn't you rather all be together?" Bree asked.

Mikkel stared at her. "Why do you always ask such strange questions?"

Bree stared back. *Why did it take me so long to figure this out?*

Later that morning Bree, Grandmother, Grandfather, and Hauk again gathered around the fire. As always, Rika worked nearby.

Grandmother was the first to ask a question. "Where does your God send people when they die?"

Ohhhh. Bree almost said it aloud. *The dark, freezing fogs.*

From the pain of being alone, Bree knew what to tell her. "Grandmother, do you like to be where people love you? When we die, we will go to be with someone who loves us forever."

Suddenly Grandmother became still, waiting to hear more, as if Bree's answer was a matter of life or death.

"Would you like to be free of what makes you so afraid?" Bree asked gently. "When Jesus grew up, He died on the cross for you. If you ask Him to forgive the wrong things that you do, He will. If you ask Him to be your Savior, He is!"

"But what is His house like?"

"It's a big house with many rooms. Jesus said He was going to get it ready for us."

"That's good?" Grandmother asked.

"It's very good. There will be no death there, no sadness or tears. We'll be clothed in white."

"Clothed in white?" Grandmother looked around the room that was always partly dark. "I would like that."

"Best of all, we'll be with Jesus. He promised to come and get us so we can be where He is. Do you want to know more about Him?"

"*Yah, takk.* Thank you, I would."

When they finished talking, Grandmother asked, "Please. Can I have the big book in my room at night?"

"I'll build a shelf for you," Grandfather promised. "I'll put the shelf next to your bed."

That night no sound disturbed Bree's sleep. When she woke somewhere near dawn, Bree was sure she had slept through Grandmother's moans. *Why didn't I hear her cry?*

Suddenly Bree felt afraid. Had something happened to her?

Quickly Bree crawled down the ladder, crept through the hallway, and slipped into Grandmother's room. The blankets were in place. Grandmother slept quietly. But one hand reached out from beneath the warm wool blankets.

On the shelf next to her bed, the big book lay open. Though Grandmother could not read what it said, her hand rested on the words of Jesus in the book of John. "I am the way, the truth, and the life. No one can come to the Father except through me."

In the light of the oil lamps, Bree saw Grandmother's look of peace.

After the early morning meal, Bree again carried scraps of food to the dogs. Whenever she appeared at the door, bowl in hand, they came running.

Kneeling down, Bree scratched behind Shadow's ears. When no one could hear, she always spoke to him in the Irish.

For the first time, Shadow turned his head and licked her wrist. "Ah, you really are my friend now," Bree said. "You're not just looking for food." His *woof* was all the yes she needed.

Though Molly no longer gave milk, Bree still talked to the cow every day. Often Bree told Molly how glad she was for the calf that would be born in the spring.

As Bree finished her chores outside the barn, the horse she had named Flurry followed close behind her. Like a small child, Flurry was curious about everything Bree did. Sometimes Bree felt she was a pest. Other times Bree loved it. She still felt the surprise of the light-colored mane with the dark stripe that ran down Flurry's back into the tail.

Reaching out, Bree stroked the mare's strong neck. Thick and powerful, it gave Flurry a proud look—one that seemed to fit this land of fjords and mountains.

Shadow and Flurry had become friends. One afternoon when Bree set out to visit Devin, the dog followed her. Behind Shadow came Flurry.

"Go back," Bree told both of them. But Flurry walked up behind her and snuffled her nose in Bree's neck. "I'm here," the mare seemed to say. "Don't forget me."

By now the sprinkling of snow that lay upon the mountains each morning no longer melted during the day. Instead, snow left a white blanket even on the stones in the river. Near the water lay the house of the jail keeper. Unlocking the door, he let Bree into Devin's cell.

The minute he was sure the jailer was gone, Dev exclaimed, "I saw her, I saw her, I saw her!"

THIRTEEN

HACKSILVER!

You saw Keely?" Bree couldn't think of anyone else who would make Dev that excited.

"She heard me playing the pipes. She rapped on the small door for passing food."

"She actually let you see her?"

Devin's grin stretched from ear to ear. "When I heard her knock, I was afraid. It was the dead of night—"

"You thought someone came to hurt you?"

Devin nodded. "I wondered about it. I waited, but then—"

Bree leaned closer.

Devin laughed with the fun of it. "Remember how Keely used to make all those funny sounds?"

"Yes!" Bree laughed as she remembered Keely's strange collection of sounds. "Which one?"

"The one she used when really tired. Remember?"

Bree laughed with him. "She meowed like a cat. It was so real I couldn't tell the difference. She had a whole range of cat noises. A meek little kitten. A howling tom cat—"

"When she was really tired," Devin prompted. "Remember? Which one?"

"The little kitten. Like a new-born kitten meowing for its mother."

Devin laughed again. "Six years it's been! Six years! I heard that meow, and I opened the door."

"You could see her?"

"She put her head down close, her face right into the opening."

"And how did she look?"

"Bree, she's the Keely we knew when she was six years old. I was afraid—"

"We were all afraid."

"Keely pushed her hand through and took mine. She shook it solemnly and said, 'Master Devin! God bless you, Master Dev.'"

As Bree reached out, offering her own hand, Devin's tears fell upon it.

"She wanted to hear all the news," he said. "I told her about Mam and Daddy. I told her how we prayed for her day after day, year after year. But when I started to tell about Adam—" Devin's voice broke.

"Someone came," Bree said. "I think Keely comes near me at night too. And she doesn't let me see her."

"One minute she was here. The next gone. Like the morning mist in the mountains, she was gone."

Bree tried to comfort him. "But you saw her for a moment. You talked with her."

"It was like the sun coming out."

"Oh, I wish I had been here." Bree ached with the loneliness of it. For Devin's sake, she tried to hold back her tears. "I wish I had seen her, too."

Then Bree could no longer hold back her tears. As she started to sob, she could not be comforted.

Devin tightened his hand on hers. "You *will* see her, Bree. You *will* talk with her."

Then he too was sobbing. When he spoke again his voice was muffled. "When we hug each other, it will not be with a wall between. It will be one big Irish hug."

Standing up, Devin opened the small door and looked out to see whether the jailer was nearby. When he sat down on the dirt floor again, he lowered his voice even more.

"Bree, are they through searching you?"

Bree sighed. "I think so. They know I came off the ship with nothing but the clothes on my back."

"You have places where you can hide something?" Devin asked.

Bree nodded. There were all kinds of hiding places in the stable. "What have you got?"

Devin knelt down and pried loose a blackened stone in the ground near where logs for the fire were kept. From a small hollow beneath the stone, he took out pieces of silver.

"Hacksilver!" Bree couldn't believe it.

Often used for barter, silver pieces were cut from larger pieces such as silver vessels or jewelry. Viking raiders shared loot among themselves by hacking up their plunder. Pieces of silver were weighed to give a common exchange.

"Where did you get hacksilver?"

"I kept it separate from the ransom money," Devin said. "Just in case."

"You got ransom money plus silver from the people of Wicklow?" In spite of their love for her, Bree couldn't imagine how they were able to give so much.

Most of the pieces of silver were small, but one piece was large and beautiful. There was also a thin silver wire looped in a circle.

"It all came from Bjorn, the cobbler in Dublin—the man who made arrangements for my trip here. He didn't want me traveling with empty pockets. He made special shoes for me."

Bending down, Devin showed Bree how Bjorn had sewn a hiding place into the top side of each shoe. The secret pocket folded in near where the leather drawstring closed around Devin's ankle. Opening a shoe again, Devin slid the thin loop of wire and some small pieces of hacksilver inside, then took them out again.

Bree picked up the largest piece of silver. "Wouldn't it be safer with you?"

"I don't think so," Devin said. "Take all of it. Hide it well. If you ever need something, you've got it."

Bree studied his face, trying to guess his thoughts. "I don't want to leave without you."

Devin grinned. "And I won't leave without you. And neither of us can leave without Keely. It's getting more and more complicated, isn't it?"

But Bree was thinking about God's provision for their need. "It's like we have new friends around the world," she said.

"And God is the best Friend of all."

"Our invisible, always-with-us Friend," Bree said softly.

On her way back to the longhouse, she thought about Grandmother. Bree felt excited about the new peace that Grandmother had. After all her bad dreams, she finally slept well at night.

As Bree started across the field, she looked up at the sheer rock wall of the mountain on the far side of the farm. Pine trees grew at the top. If someone looked out between those trees, she would be able to see the fjord, the Aurland River, and the mountains beyond. That person could see the entire Aurland valley, including the farm where Mikkel and his family lived.

Now Bree wondered, *Does Keely ever come to that high spot? Does she look down on us and see what I'm doing?*

It gave Bree a warm feeling, as if Keely were with her even when Bree couldn't see her. Yet it bothered Bree too. *If Keely knows where I live, why doesn't she find me? I'm her sister! Doesn't she want to talk to me?*

As soon as Bree reached the barn, she found a hiding place. Carefully she tucked Dev's treasure into a crack in the wall close to where she slept. Whenever Bree thought about the silver, she wondered how to use it best. And now she felt excited. With Grandmother sleeping well, she could search for Keely!

But that night the winds of winter howled down the fjord. The storm and the snows that came with it kept Bree close to the longhouse. Most difficult of all was knowing that Keely had to be somewhere nearby. Close enough to walk, yet too far to make her way through the snow.

When Bree went to the river for water, a layer of ice had formed around the rocks. Bree used a bucket to break an opening and dip the water out. The next day the ice extended farther into the stream. Then both the fjord and the river were completely frozen over.

Rika told Bree not to mind. The men would haul all the water for both people and animals. They would carry it in barrels from a spring some distance away. The work was heavy—too heavy for a girl.

But Bree *did* mind. Her walks to the river had given her a few moments of freedom. During her first weeks in Aurland she had watched the gold light of morning touch the mountains and reach into the valley on both sides of the river. In those moments she remembered God's promises to her. Though other people saw her as a slave, she was the daughter of a King.

Soon Rika said that more snow had already fallen than they sometimes had for an entire winter. The people who lived close to each other were joined by pathways through the snow. Bree followed those paths to the jailhouse. There she heard Dev coughing.

At first Devin brushed aside Bree's concern about his cough. Then he could no longer hide it. When he started coughing, he could not stop.

With each cough Bree grew more upset. Stalking away from the jail, she searched for Mikkel. She found him down by the fjord, working on his ship.

"You've got to get my brother out of there!" Bree stormed as she walked into the boathouse.

"Out of jail?" Mikkel's voice was hard.

"It's cold. It's damp. It stinks. Dev will die in that hole."

FOURTEEN

A MATTER OF TRUST

Mikkel stood next to his longship. Chips of wood lay on the ground, and shelves held the tools of his trade. Deep inside, Mikkel felt scared for Devin, but he shrugged and let his voice sound careless. "If Devin dies, he dies."

Anger filled Bree's face. "How can you be so cruel? It's your fault that he's there."

"No," Mikkel said. "It's Devin's fault that he's there. I let him go, and he walked back into the trap. Who else in the whole earth would be foolish enough to do that?"

"It's not foolishness," Bree said. "Not if you love someone." Tears welled up in her eyes. Quickly she blinked them away, but a tear slid down her cheek. "My brother loves me."

If there was anything Mikkel hated, it was watching Bree cry. Most of the time she managed herself better than that. He would rather see her anger spill over with every word. Though he didn't like it, Mikkel had grown used to that.

Now he put down the axe he had picked up just before Bree came. Usually his hands were steady. From the time Mikkel was very young he had used an axe. By now he was proud of his work. Watching Bree cry upset him. One slip because she was here, and he could spoil the boards he had worked so hard to make perfect.

"My brother works with my daddy—" Bree went on, and her voice was steady again.

"Devin is a good shipbuilder?"

"He's good with his hands," Bree said. "He could be your blacksmith, make rivets—"

Mikkel looked down at the ship he was building. He too had worked with his father since he was old enough to handle tools. By now he knew shipbuilding well. He and his men were overlapping the long, wedge-shaped pieces of wood used in a clinker-built ship.

Bree was smart enough to know what he needed—countless rivets to hold those boards together. Each of those rivets had to be made by a blacksmith.

Looking up, Mikkel saw Bree watching him. "You and Devin think of nothing but running away. You don't let yourself like it here."

As though surprised that he understood, Bree stared at him. "That's true," she said softly. "We think of nothing but being together. We're a family, Mikkel. We will always hope that we can be a family again."

Like a sword piercing his soul, Mikkel felt the hurt of it. As Bree waited for his answer, Mikkel's father and brother entered the boathouse.

"You want Devin to work for you?" Sigurd asked Mikkel, clearly puzzled by the turn of events. "First you capture him. Then you set him free. Then you force me to jail him for his own protection. If he works for you, how will you treat him?"

"With fairness."

"There's something I don't understand." Sigurd turned to Bree. "How does your brother feel about working for my son?"

"I haven't asked him yet," Bree said.

"This is your plan and Mikkel's? Why?"

"My brother is coughing. I don't want him to die."

"And he will be better off in the cold, working in a blacksmith shop?"

"My mam is known as a woman with healing in her hands. Mam knows that cough. She says it can become the cough of someone who wastes away."

"What else does your mother say?"

"That someone who coughs like that should get fresh

air. People in the Wicklow Mountains respect Mam's words. So do I."

"And you, Bree," Sigurd said. "Are you also known as a healer?"

"Oh, no!" Bree exclaimed. "Only God heals. I just watched my mother. That's the way we do it in Ireland."

"Mikkel?" Sigurd asked. "Can you keep that temper of yours under control?"

A spark of anger lit Mikkel's insides. But then he forced himself to let it go. "Yes," he said, respect in his voice. "I will keep my anger under control."

As Sigurd searched his face, Mikkel met his gaze. Whatever Sigurd saw there, he seemed pleased. Mikkel felt relieved.

"Each night Devin must return to the jail," Sigurd said. "But tell the jailer to keep him in his house instead of that hole he calls a cell. Tell him to feed Devin well and give him enough blankets to keep him warm."

When Mikkel and Bree set off to see Devin, they walked across the snow-covered ground in silence. Mikkel knew Bree was still upset with him.

It wasn't hard to guess that Bree was afraid to speak. Mikkel could see questions all over her face. *She's wondering about me. She's wondering if I'll change my mind, in spite of what I said to my father.*

But Mikkel had his own questions. *Will Devin be willing to work for me?*

"Your brother Devin," Mikkel said. "Will he promise to not run away?"

Inside her mittens Bree's fists clenched, as though the pain of her own promise struck her a new blow. When she unknotted them and nodded slightly, Mikkel knew she was saying yes.

"Dev will hate the promise as much as I do," she said. "But you must take care of him, or you'll lose a good worker to the grave that you fear."

As though she had struck him, Mikkel stepped back. *How did she know?* Sometimes it seemed Bree could see right inside of him to the feelings he wanted to hide.

"I'll take care of him," Mikkel said. "But only if he takes care himself."

When the jailer opened his door, Mikkel spoke to him. "My father says I'm to speak to your prisoner. If he is willing to work for me during the day—"

The jail keeper nodded. "I am to release him to your care."

"And I will see that he is returned to you each night."

Going out ahead of them, the jailer knocked on the small door used to give Devin food. Devin opened the door at once. When he glanced through the opening, his eyes widened at the sight of Mikkel.

"My father, Sigurd, the mighty chieftain of the Aurland Fjord, has a question for you," Mikkel said solemnly. "Would you choose to work for me during the day?"

Devin glanced at Bree. Barely moving her head, she nodded.

"Yes," Devin said.

"Would you promise to not run away?"

Again Devin glanced toward Bree. "I promise to not run away during the hours I work for you."

But Mikkel caught the change in words. "How foolish do you think I am? I'm asking you to make a promise because I know your sister keeps her promises. Do you?"

Devin grinned. "If I make them."

Mikkel did not think it was funny. "The promise is this. You will not run away. You will not try to escape. I will be able to trust you to do good work. And you will wait in Aurland for the *ting*—the assembly of freemen—to make its decision."

Watching, Mikkel saw Devin swallow hard. He too took a promise seriously. It was just as hard for him as it had been for Bree.

Mikkel thought about it. He knew the *ting* well enough to know that their decisions were just and fair. But Devin didn't. He had no idea what awaited him.

"I need time to think about it," Devin said.

"Dev—"

"No, Bree. I have to think about this."

As Bree sighed, Mikkel saw her face. Clearly she was unhappy. No doubt she wondered if he and his father would change their minds, giving Devin no second chance.

Slowly Bree wrapped her scarf around her head. "Courage to win, Dev," she said, reaching her hand through the small opening. When she and the jailer left, Mikkel stayed with Devin.

"You do not trust me," Mikkel said.

His head bowed, Devin only nodded.

"I want to earn your trust," Mikkel said quietly.

"Earn my trust?" Through the small opening Devin looked up, searching Mikkel's face. "How can you possibly earn my trust?"

"My father is a just and fair man. I want to learn to be wise, the way my father is."

"And you would practice on me?" Devin's voice was bitter.

Mikkel's voice was steady. "I will practice on you." Like Bree, he reached his hand through the opening, but Devin did not take it.

His hand still extended, Mikkel waited. Devin looked away, then finally said, "I have to think."

"Think!" Mikkel stared at him. "Don't you know you have no other choice?" Mikkel had seen what happened to people who coughed for a long time and kept growing weaker. It frightened him. The worst of it was that he liked Bree's brother. Yet from the moment they met they had been enemies.

As Mikkel turned to go, Devin spoke quickly. "Please. Can Bree come see me tomorrow?"

Mikkel nodded, but turned quickly away. When he caught up to Bree, he said, "Your brother wants to see you tomorrow. Alone."

Bree smiled her relief. "Without you listening."

Mikkel shook his head. Sometimes he resented her honesty. Other times he felt wonder. "You Irish! You have nothing going for you, but you think you hold the world."

Bree lifted her chin. "We do."

On the way back to the longhouse, she asked Mikkel what Devin said. Unwilling to tell her more, Mikkel spat out four words. "We talked about trust."

FIFTEEN

A PLACE APART

Trust. As Bree walked to see Devin the next day, she thought about it.

Before meeting Mikkel, she had taken trust for granted. Since coming to know him, she had asked herself countless times, "Can I trust what Mikkel says?"

For as long as Bree could remember, she had known that she could trust her brother Devin, her father, her mother, their closest neighbors and friends. Bree had also known she could trust Tully, the special friend she thought she had rescued that day in Ireland. But then the person she thought was Tully proved to be Mikkel.

Trust. As Bree walked across the frozen ground, she felt the cold rising from the ice.

Trust. Once broken, everything froze—like chunks of ice—between people. Mikkel had broken trust with the Viking raid. He had broken the trust Devin had placed in the man who promised safe passage. Mikkel had even broken trust by taking the ransom money and acting in a way that sent Devin to jail.

But deep inside, Bree felt sure that Mikkel was still hiding something even worse from his father. *What does Dev know that I don't know?*

When Bree reached the jailhouse, the jail keeper let her inside Devin's cell. As Bree sat down on the three-legged stool, Devin cracked open the small door in the wall. Together they waited until the sound of the jailer's footsteps faded away.

Then Devin spoke quickly. "I saw your face last night. I listened to your plan to get me out of here during the day. It's a good one, and my cough isn't nearly as bad as you think. But I'm afraid to work for Mikkel."

"You think he'll hurt you?"

Devin shook his head. "Not while his father is around."

"No slipped tool? No accident?"

"I'll be careful of it, but I don't think so. What I'm really afraid of is myself, and what I know."

"About Mikkel." Bree watched her brother's eyes. Devin knew people. He sensed truth. And he sensed when it wasn't there.

"When I was in Dublin, I met a shoemaker named Bjorn. He is a good and kind Norwegian. He came from the Aurland Fjord, and his best friend here is Mikkel's father, Sigurd. Mikkel brought him trade goods. Bjorn paid him with silver and the shoes that Sigurd wanted to buy. And then—"

Devin shook his head, as if even yet he didn't want to believe what had happened.

"And then?" Bree asked.

"Mikkel stole a bag of valuable silver coins."

Bree stared at Devin. "Mikkel traded with his father's best friend, then stole from him?"

Devin nodded. "And now Mikkel asks me to trust him. 'I want to be worthy of trust,' he says."

"I knew it, I knew it, I knew it!" Bree said.

"You knew what?"

"That Mikkel has been hiding something from his father. Something that would upset his father even more than the raid on Glendalough."

"Bjorn the shoemaker hated the raid. He hated what Mikkel had done. He knew it would displease Mikkel's father. Bjorn is the one who arranged for my safe passage."

"The bag of silver coins—I've seen it!" Bree said. "Mikkel had three bags of coins. I saw him give only one to his father."

"And the other two bags?"

Bree thought about it. "One must be treasure he stole

from Glendalough. The gifts that pilgrims brought to the monastery."

"And the other bag?"

"From what you say, it must be the silver coins that belong to Bjorn."

"If it is, it's valuable. Before Bjorn became a shoemaker in Dublin, he traveled the world in Viking ships. He saved coins from faraway places. Many of them are Arabic. And Bjorn said, 'If you can manage to separate Mikkel from my coins and return them to me, I'll give you a reward.'"

Bree stared at her brother. "Oh, Dev, you can't say a word. Mikkel will do anything to keep his father from knowing."

"But what if I forget?" Devin asked. "You want me to work for Mikkel, to get out of this hole—" Devin looked around. "But what if he makes me really angry? What if I say something that gives away what I know?"

When Bree's stomach started to churn, she tried to pay no attention. But then, filled with terror, she could only stare at her brother. She felt sure of one thing. If he didn't get out, his cough would get worse. It could even kill him. But if he did leave here to work for Mikkel, what would happen?

"If Mikkel knows that you know—" she said.

Suddenly Bree could no longer ignore her stomach.

Standing up, she ran for the door. She barely made it to the nearest snow bank before she was sick.

When she returned to Devin's cell, the jailer wouldn't let her back in. The moment he left, Bree went to the small door for passing food.

"Dev, does anyone besides you know that Mikkel stole from Bjorn?"

When her brother shook his head, Bree spoke even more softly. "Dev, your life is in danger."

As Bree walked back to the longhouse, she felt sick at heart. The more she found out about Mikkel, the more he upset her. At times he was a very likeable person. At other times he made Bree so angry that she could barely handle it. In those terrible moments, she knew she had no choice but to forgive Mikkel. But she quite regularly told God, "Seventy times seven? I have to choose to forgive him that often? I've already lost count!"

With the wrong between them building up, Bree felt sure she would never come to a place where she could respect Mikkel.

During the evening meal, Bree watched Grandmother. She was like a different person—peaceful now by day and by night. But then Bree noticed Mikkel's brother again. Sitting at one end of a long bench, Cort seemed to set himself apart. Though with the family, he seldom talked.

When Rika or Sigurd tried to draw him in, Cort resisted even them. Like a shadow, he stayed around the edges of the family. Quiet. Silent.

Lurking, Bree decided. *There, but not really. Never a real part of the circle.*

When he wanted, Cort knew how to speak. *Why doesn't he take part?* Bree wondered. *Why do his eyes seem shadowed and far away?*

But then Bree knew she was mistaken. When Cort looked at Mikkel, his eyes were not shadowed or far away. The fire of resentment burned there.

Now Mikkel turned to Bree. "What did Devin say?"

"He hasn't decided yet." Bree turned away. It would take some time to get used to looking at Mikkel again. She didn't know if she could manage, knowing what she now knew.

Mikkel tried to tease her out of her mood. "Tell your brother I'd be a good lad to work for."

Lad. That's what Bree called the Irish boys she knew. Bree wouldn't honor Mikkel with the word. She had her own thoughts about someone like Mikkel, and she could speak none of them aloud.

Trust! Mikkel asks Dev to trust him?

Bree stalked over to the fire and began dishing up food. Tonight they were having pork. Pork cooked to perfection by Rika until the scent of it filled the longhouse.

But Bree searched through every piece until she found

one as tough as the shoes on her feet. When she dished up Mikkel's portion, that was the piece she gave him.

The next morning Mikkel told Bree, "Go back to Devin. I need a blacksmith."

When Bree said no, Mikkel said, "You are a slave. You can't say you won't talk to your brother."

"It's between you and Dev," Bree told him.

"You want me to go talk to him again?"

Bree shrugged as though she didn't care. "How much do you need a blacksmith? Would you rather have a silversmith?"

"Like who?" Mikkel sounded careful now.

"Like someone who has already begun to learn—an apprentice who knows some of the great silver work. The patterns of—"

"Ireland?" Mikkel guessed. "Would that silversmith by any chance be you?"

"Well—" Bree said cautiously. "I was just starting to learn from the silversmith at the monastery."

"And you just happen to know how to melt coins down and make them into something valuable?"

"Well—" Bree said again. She didn't want to sound too eager, or too skillful. Nor did she want to lie—

But Mikkel was already running with the idea. "If I found a silversmith, he could teach you what you don't know. Between the two of you, you could make me a wealthy man—"

"Yes," Bree answered softly. She did her best to hide her thoughts, but the moment Mikkel was gone, she laughed out loud. It was always Mikkel's greed that won. That and his need to impress others. *And maybe I'll find out where you hid that valuable hoard of coins you stole.*

Bree never heard how Mikkel convinced Devin to work for him. She only knew that on days when a storm did not keep everyone inside, Mikkel went to get him.

More than once, Bree watched Mikkel and Devin as they crossed the field on a path through the snow. Sometimes they walked together without speaking. Other times they talked as if they were friends. And still other times, one or both of them looked stiff with anger. On those days Bree felt afraid.

"What do you and Mikkel talk about?" she asked Devin one day. Her brother only grinned.

By asking among the Irish slaves, Mikkel soon found a silversmith. His name was Neece, and his home in Ireland lay close to the sea. In a small building away from the longhouse, Neece set up a crucible for melting down coins. When Mikkel found the right tools, Neece and Bree were ready to work.

On the days when Rika had an older woman help with the weaving, Bree worked with Neece. She quickly found he was a gifted silversmith and willing to teach her all he knew. Step by step, Neece showed Bree how to twist ropes of silver into the patterns for which the Irish were famous.

As Bree learned from Neece, her plan started to take shape. Alone in the stable at night, she took out the pieces of hacksilver. By the light of the oil lamp she tried to decide what to do with them. How could she turn the silver into something that would be worth even more?

Often Bree looked at the small, straight pieces and the loop of fine thin wire. The nicest piece of all seemed to be cut from the arc of a circle. Along the outer edge it had a braided design.

If the assembly of freemen did not return the ransom money to Devin, he needed a way to get out of jail. In order to be free, she would need ransom money. And they also needed to free Keely.

Somehow Bree was going to find a way for all of them to get home. As soon as there was a break in the weather, she'd look for her sister again. If there was a full moon, she could even search at night.

When Sigurd came in from a cold winter morning, he walked with a heavy step. Instead of sitting down, he asked the family to go outdoors. As Bree stayed by the fire, he looked back and said, "You, too, Bree."

Outside, where the light was better, Sigurd said, "I must tell you something."

Standing apart from the rest of them, he held out his right hand.

Rika gasped. "Oh, no!"

Cort took one look and backed off. Usually quiet, he surprised Bree by speaking. "Oh, Father!"

Then it was Mikkel's turn. Moving forward, he too stared at the hand. When he stepped away, Bree saw tears in his eyes.

Neither of the grandparents needed to look. They knew. And so did Bree. She had often heard her mother speak of the disease known as leprosy. It had been present in Ireland from early times. In his travels had Sigurd somehow come in contact with a leper?

"Today I must separate myself from you," Sigurd said. "Today I must move to a place apart. There I will wait for my fate."

When Rika began crying, she held her hands over her mouth, trying to hide her sobs. But Grandmother went to her, put her arms around Rika, and held her.

Like a small bird hopping from branch to branch, Bree's thoughts scattered in every direction. In Ireland too this disease afflicted people. There too it started with small lumps and a thickening of the skin. And then, as time went on, it affected a finger, toe, hand, or foot.

"Unclean!" Sigurd whispered as though unable to speak the word aloud. "I am unclean!"

Then, moving back still farther from them, Sigurd spoke with the strength that had always marked him. "Take care of each other, my family. Be honest with all people. Be fair." As though thinking of Devin, his gaze rested on Bree.

"Cort, I will help you from afar, but in all matters of law and business, you are now head of this family."

Finally Sigurd turned to his youngest son. "I'm sorry, Mikkel. When the wind blows fair, you must go alone."

Alone! Like a heavy weight, the word dropped among them. For Sigurd would be the most alone of them all.

His head bowed, he turned away. His step was slow and sorrowful as he walked to a small building set apart from the rest. Slowly he opened the door, stepped inside, and shut the door behind him.

Only then did Rika cry out. "Leprosy! How could such a good man have leprosy?"

SIXTEEN

CHRISTMAS MORNING

All that day, Bree kept thinking about Sigurd. In the Bible, lepers were expected to call out, "Unclean! Unclean!" and warn people away. It frightened Bree.

When it was time for the evening meal, Rika said, "You must feed Sigurd."

"I'm afraid," Bree told her. She didn't want to touch Sigurd's dishes. "What if I get leprosy?"

But Rika was also afraid. "If I get leprosy, who will care for Grandmother? Who will care for the other older women and the children? They all depend on me."

Rika spoke truth. Who could possibly take her place?

When the family gathered for their evening meal, Rika, Cort, Mikkel, and the grandparents sat quietly. All of them were stunned by Sigurd's bad news. Bree still felt afraid. Then as she served the family, she remembered a story she had learned.

"Please," Bree asked Rika. "Can I tell you a story in the Bible?"

Bree had grown used to talking with Rika and the grandparents, but now she wondered what Mikkel and Cort would say. Turning so she didn't have to look at them, Bree spoke to Rika instead.

"A long time ago there was a man named Naaman who commanded the armies of his king. But Naaman had a contagious skin disease."

"Leprosy?" Rika barely breathed the dreaded word.

But Bree went on. "When Naaman's army raided another country a young girl was taken captive. She became a servant to Naaman's wife. One day the girl said, 'I wish my master would go see the prophet Elisha. He would heal my master.' When Naaman went, Elisha said, 'Go and wash yourself seven times in the Jordan River. You will be healed of leprosy.'"

"And Naaman was healed?" Grandfather asked.

"Not at first. Naaman became angry and didn't want to go. He said, 'I thought the prophet would surely come out to meet me! I expected him to wave his hand over the leprosy and call on the name of the Lord his God!' Aren't the two rivers of Damascus better than all the rivers of Israel put together?'"

"I don't understand," Grandmother said.

Bree thought for a moment, wondering what to say. But Rika, Cort, Mikkel, and the grandparents waited. Finally Bree said, "It was as if Naaman asked, 'Aren't two rivers in the Aurland Fjord better than all the rivers of Ireland? Why do I have to wash in an Irish river?'"

Grandmother nodded her understanding, but a smile lurked in Grandfather's eyes. "Naaman was angry," Grandfather said. "So he wasn't healed?"

"His officers tried to reason with him. They said, 'If the prophet told you to do some great thing, wouldn't you do it? So why not obey him when he says, 'Wash and be healed'?"

"And what happened?" This time it was Mikkel who asked.

"Naaman dipped himself seven times in the Jordan River. His flesh became healthy. He was healed!"

"Ahhhh!" Rika's voice was filled with satisfaction. For the first time that day she looked as if there might be hope. "So who will tell Sigurd the story from the Bible?"

Without waiting for an answer, Rika decided what to do. "You, Bree. You tell Sigurd the story."

But Grandmother looked at Grandfather. "Tell Bree," Grandmother said.

With a new light in his eyes and the half smile Bree had seen before, Grandfather leaned forward. "A long time ago a wise man walked through these mountains," he said.

"We scoffed at the stories he told about Jesus. Why would a god be so loving and kind? But after the man left, we were sorry we laughed. We prayed that if this man spoke truth about Jesus, someone would come and teach us."

"You came, Bree," Grandmother said.

Bree stared at her. "I came?"

"You came," Grandfather echoed.

As the strangeness of it struck Bree, she felt overwhelmed. Then she felt the wonder of it. *God can use something as terrible as slavery for good?*

For an instant Bree glanced at Mikkel and found him watching her. She looked away just as quickly. She couldn't help but wonder about the strange expression in his eyes.

"If I had listened long ago, my son would have known about your Jesus," Grandfather said. "Now I want to be the one to tell Sigurd."

The next day Grandfather stood outside in the snow, telling the story of Naaman the leper. Sigurd stood in the doorway of the small building and listened. When Grandfather finished, Sigurd shook his head.

"No, no!" His voice was filled with discouragement. "It is just a story. No one is ever healed of leprosy."

But Grandfather did not give up. In the days that followed, he often stood in the snow, talking to his son. At mealtimes Grandfather bowed his head to thank God for their food. And he always prayed for Sigurd.

When Gna came to the door, she carried a large basket. Standing in front of the loom where it leaned against the wall, Bree did not turn. She only hoped that Gna would not notice her.

As Rika welcomed her, Gna set the basket down on the large flat stones around the fire.

"I bring you food for strength, food for healing," she said. "And I will offer sacrifices to the gods."

Rika bowed her head in respect. "Thank you, Gna."

"Our honorable chieftain, Sigurd, how is he?" the girl asked.

"The disease on his skin grows."

Gna backed away. "And you?" she asked. "Is your skin clean?"

"My skin is clean." Rika's voice sounded calm, but now Bree knew her well enough to guess the turmoil within.

"You must tell me if it changes," Gna said.

Rika nodded. "I know."

"We do not want a plague," Gna said.

"No."

"It would spread from one man, one woman to the next. From one farm, one—"

"I know, Gna. We have taken every precaution. Sigurd lives in a place apart. No one—not even Mikkel, nor I— goes close."

"But food? Who brings his food? Who brings his water? And who carries his dishes away?"

Her heart in her throat, Bree tried to step deeper into the shadows. But Gna had already noticed her.

"Bree. It is Bree, isn't it? She is the cause of all your sorrow. She is the one who brings a curse upon your house."

"No!" Rika exclaimed.

"She is the one who must be cast to the winds, sent into the next storm—"

"No!" Rika said again.

"If she is innocent, she will come back safe. If she is not—"

"No!" Rika's usually calm face was flushed with anger. "Bree has brought blessing upon my house."

Gna stepped back. In her white face, her blue eyes seemed like burning embers. "You dare to question what I say?"

Whirling around, Gna headed for the door. She did not look back.

When Gna was gone, Rika sank down on the flat stones around the long hearth. Her hands were shaking as she held them out over the embers. Then she put her hands to her face, covering her eyes as Sigurd had the first night Bree was there. For the second time since coming there, Bree saw Rika cry.

When finally her sobbing stopped, Bree sat down nearby. "Gna hates you," Rika said.

"Because of the goat?" When Bree told about the billy goat, Rika smiled.

"It's never good to make fun of someone. Did you and Mikkel do that?"

"We laughed," Bree said. "It slipped out."

Rika thought for a moment. "Gna could have laughed about it herself. It would have all come right."

Bree understood. "As if we shared something between us."

"But Gna hates you for another reason too. Hauk no longer goes to the sacred grove. When Hauk speaks, people listen. What he does, other people do."

When Bree left for the night, she stopped at the door to the barn and looked back. Rika sat quietly now, but the tears were still wet on her cheeks. "Be careful, Bree," she said. "Gna is not kind. Be very careful."

Deep in the mound of hay, covered by the warm wool blanket, Bree woke in the middle of the night. First she heard the creak of timbers. The stamp of a horse in the stall. But then Bree wondered if there was something more.

Was that the wind under the eaves? Or someone outside again?

Barely breathing, Bree listened. Was it the crunch that came when someone walked on very cold snow?

Who is it? Who walks there at night? What does it mean?

I'm imagining things, Bree told herself. But something

she couldn't name made her afraid. For the rest of the night Bree lay awake.

On days when it was too cold to work in the boathouse, the men mended harnesses or tools. Sometimes they played chess before the fire. Around them, children gathered to play their own games and keep warm. And always the women sewed, or mended, or worked at the loom. When they finished the many long strips of cloth, they would sew them together to make the sail for Mikkel.

At times Bree thought she could not bear to look at another piece of yarn. At other times she remembered how a Viking sail looked—large and majestic, beautiful and filled with wind.

In the few times when Bree had a free moment, she put on her warm wool clothing and slipped outside. Sometimes people strapped small pieces of bone to the bottom of their shoes and skated where the ice was free of snow. More often, people skied when they went places. At first Bree thought the long narrow sticks on their feet looked strange. But when she saw how quickly Mikkel and Cort glided across the snow, Bree wished she could try.

Then she wished for the full moon. A full moon, a clear sky, and weather in which she could search for her sister. But why didn't Keely find her?

Keely, you know where I am, Bree thought more than once. *Why don't you come here? I'm your sister! Don't you want to see me?*

In December Bree kept track of the days and thought about Christmas. What would it mean to not be able to go to church, light candles, or sing the songs of Christmas? This year she especially wanted to celebrate with Keely.

Bree still felt that her sister was very near. Close by, yet hidden away. There was one direction where Bree hadn't been able to search. That was where she'd go, first chance she got.

If I could ski like Mikkel on top of the snow—if I could— but Bree couldn't, and even three or four miles might be a long way in deep snow.

Growing up in the Wicklow Mountains, Bree knew how dangerous mountains could be for an inexperienced climber. Before the snows came, she had studied the sides of the mountains around her. Up and down the fjord there were long narrow openings or wide deep hollows. With snow deep upon the land Bree had to ask herself, *Where would the ground be solid beneath me?* Filled and hidden by snow, the dangers became too big to risk.

But she and Dev could celebrate Christmas.

"Please," Bree said to Rika on Christmas morning.

"This is the special day when we celebrate the birth of Jesus. May I visit my brother?"

"If you were home, what would you do?" Rika asked.

Bree thought for a moment. If she said she went to church, someone might expect her to go to the sacred grove.

"We would light candles," Bree told Rika instead. "They're a symbol for us."

Taking a key from her belt, Rika unlocked a chest and surprised Bree by taking out a candle. Usually the family used lamps because oil was plentiful.

"When you celebrate with your brother, light the candle," Rika said. "And you celebrate by eating too?" Taking out a basket, Rika packed a few small treats.

The blacksmith shop where Devin worked was set off from the house, and Bree followed the path through the snow. As she drew near the smithy, Bree heard the pound of the hammer. Then she heard the sound of singing. Her brother was singing?

True, he had a better voice than she. He could sing to someone other than a cow. But it told Bree that Dev was lonesome, too.

Together they gathered around the warmth of the smithy fire. Together they repeated every promise they remembered about Jesus being the light of the world. Then in the light of the candle, Bree told Dev about the words that had changed how she felt about everything— "You will know the truth, and the truth will set you free."

Though a slave, Bree had never felt more free than in that moment.

"You know," Devin said. "I've had a lot of time to think while I'm pounding a hammer. It seems like a mistake that we were captured by Vikings. But was it really a mistake? If we believe God protects us, we need to ask, 'Why does He want us here?'"

"Mikkel wanted to know what God's protection is," Bree said.

"He did? Watch out! Maybe Mikkel wants protection for his next voyage."

"Do you suppose he'll ever change?" Bree asked.

Devin grinned. "If he has the right friends."

"I keep thinking about Sigurd," Bree said. "if he could speak at the assembly of freemen, he would put in a good word for you."

The bad news about their chieftain's leprosy had spread quickly through the surrounding fjords and mountains. "What if Sigurd would be healed?" Devin asked now. "What if God decided to do that, not just to help me, but to help the people who don't know Him? It would be a miracle."

Bree smiled. "A miracle, all right. But long before we were born God started doing miracles."

When Bree stood up to leave, she had Christmas in her heart. Devin had Christmas in both his eyes and his smile.

SEVENTEEN

THE STORYTELLER

Between snowfalls Mikkel tromped down the new path to the boathouse. Whenever possible, he and the men worked on the partly built ship. As Mikkel smoothed the wood, he dreamed of far places and felt eager for spring to come. *When the wind blows fair, I'll be gone.*

Most days he walked to the jailhouse and brought Devin to the blacksmith shop. There, warmed by the fire at which he worked, Devin made rivets—metal bolts with a head on one end. The rivets would hold the long overlapping boards of the ship together.

To Mikkel's secret relief, Devin no longer coughed. Now, as Mikkel started back to the house, he heard laughter from the smithy. *Laughter?* Wasn't Devin working as he should? In order to finish his ship, Mikkel needed countless rivets.

Changing his direction, Mikkel walked that way. Above the laughter came the pound, pound, pound of the hammer.

Good, Mikkel thought. They did not have time to waste. But then the hammer stopped.

"No! You can't come that close. Move back or you won't be safe."

It was Devin speaking. Who was he talking to? The children who lived here in winter? Children who worked as they could because there wasn't enough food deep in the mountains? Staying out of sight, Mikkel listened.

"There. That's good," Devin said. "I will not tell a story if you come too close."

Tell a story? Mikkel asked himself. *My blacksmith fills my smithy with his stories?*

But instead of words, Mikkel heard the whoosh of bellows. Bellows fanning the flames, making the iron red hot so it could be worked.

And then Devin began speaking again. Between blows of the hammer, he told a story Mikkel had never heard. A story about a brother and sister playing in the green fields of Ireland.

Here and there came the soft, pleased sigh of a child. Now and then someone clapped. But always the blow of the hammer kept ringing. How could Devin work and talk at the same time?

Then Mikkel found himself caught up in the story. This was not just any tale, but the story of a brother and sister living in mountains where mists came and mists went and the land stayed green forever. Suddenly Mikkel knew the story was true.

At first Mikkel wanted to walk around the wall and stop the story. Then he wanted to hear it end. Staying out of sight, Mikkel crept closer.

Bree and Devin. That's who the brother and sister were. Then through the laughter of the children who listened, Mikkel felt sad. *That's the way it was with Ivar and me. That's what I lost when Ivar died at sea.*

When tears welled up in his eyes, Mikkel brushed them away. Not for anything would he show how much he missed his favorite brother.

As young children they had always played together. At night around the fire, they shared laughter and secrets. Then, as though still seeing those times, Mikkel saw his brother Cort. Always left out. Always at the edge of whatever Ivar and Mikkel did.

No wonder Cort dislikes me, Mikkel thought. *Have I always gone my own way without him? Will I someday be sorry for that too?*

Again Mikkel thought about the way Bree and Devin treated each other. *Separated by hardship—by distance, by me*

—Mikkel had to admit it. *But both took life or death risks to take care of each other. Could Cort ever love me that way?*

Mikkel tried to push the thought aside, but couldn't. *I'm proud of my father and mother. I was proud of Ivar. I wish I could be proud of Cort.*

But then, Mikkel had to be honest with himself. *Maybe I must first be able to respect myself. But how?*

Somehow he had managed to hide his darkest secret from his father. But he couldn't hide that secret from himself.

Then as he started to slip away, Mikkel saw his brother. Cort was also standing just out of sight of Devin and the children. He too was listening.

And now Mikkel knew what he needed to do. *I'm going to change,* he promised himself. But then, deep inside, Mikkel wondered if he really could.

EIGHTEEN

TROUBLEMAKER

When Devin turned fifteen, he and Bree celebrated again, this time by telling each other funny stories. But one week later, when Mikkel also turned fifteen, Bree did not feel like celebrating. She only thought about Mikkel's dark secret. Whenever she recalled the stolen bag of coins, Bree remembered its danger to her brother.

Each morning Mikkel gave her and Neece the coins he wanted them to melt down. Bree couldn't tell if these came from the raid at Glendalough or Mikkel's theft from his father's friend in Dublin. Neither Bree nor Neece had any idea where Mikkel hid his valuable hoard.

Often Bree thought about the hacksilver Dev had given her. "Hide it well," he said, and Bree had. As Neece taught her how to shape jewelry, Bree learned ways to turn silver into something even more valuable. *If I make something beautiful—if I can somehow sell it—*

One afternoon Bree told the silversmith what she wanted to try.

"No, Bree," he said at first. "It could make trouble."

Then Neece changed his mind. He understood how Bree felt. He too wanted to be free. But when Neece decided to help Bree, he warned her. "You must be very careful. If anyone sees what you're doing, there will be trouble."

Since the first day she worked with him, Bree had watched and learned all she could. Now Neece showed her how to make a neckring—a thin silver band, molded and shaped with great care. A pendant hung by a loop from the band.

"It's beautiful!" Bree exclaimed.

Neece smiled. "Someday you will make neckrings just as beautiful."

But Bree didn't want to wait. That night she took the pieces of hacksilver from hiding. In the light of the oil lamp she studied the thin wire and small bits and pieces. If she kept the beautifully woven pattern of the largest piece of silver, she could shape it into a pendant. She only needed to make the silver loop that went around a woman's neck.

The next day Bree finished Mikkel's work and then started making her own jewelry. Holding out the piece she wanted for a pendant, Bree used a hammer to pound the bits of hacksilver into a long, flat piece. After rolling that silver into a smooth unbroken line, she polished it into a sparkling strand.

Then Neece showed Bree how to use the strand in a neckring that would look like a circular braid. Still working together, they shaped the large, beautifully designed piece of hacksilver into a pendant. Then Bree attached the pendant to the silver loop.

When she finished, the neckring was more beautiful than Bree ever dreamed possible. Even Neece was excited about the unusual beauty of what they had created.

"It's the kind of jewelry men give their wives to display their wealth," he said.

As Bree tucked their creation into a hiding place, she could hardly wait to show it to Devin. But Neece reminded Bree, "Be very, very careful."

Then the day came. *Full moon tonight,* Bree thought during a break in the weather. Tonight she would search for Keely. But first, since Mikkel and Devin were not working that day, Bree asked if she could visit her brother.

Feeling like royalty instead of a slave, Bree clasped the silver ring around her neck, then hid it beneath her cloak. With a light heart she followed one of the snowy paths that wound between houses to the jail.

Today Bree wore pride around her neck—the pride of knowing that even if the assembly of freemen didn't return the ransom, she had a way to free her brother. Today Bree would show Dev the neckring, then hide it again until needed.

The afternoon was warm in the shelter of the mountain. As Bree walked, she pulled open her cloak. When she felt the ring around her neck, she wished she could see the sparkle of the silver strand. Instead, she saw Gna coming around a house ahead of her.

Quickly Bree turned aside, taking a different path to avoid the girl. But Gna also changed paths. When she stood directly in front of her, Bree had no choice but to stop.

At first Gna simply looked Bree in the eyes. Then she moved closer for a better look. "Your neckring!" she exclaimed.

Bree stepped back, out of reach.

"Where did you get it?"

Backing up even farther, Bree prepared to run.

"How can a slave girl have a neckring like that? You stole it!"

"No!" Bree exclaimed. "I didn't!"

Gna's scoffing laugh seemed to echo from the mountainside. Suddenly she called out to a man working nearby. "This thief stole my neckring!"

Bree stared at her. "*Your* neckring?"

Then with horror Bree realized that one person after

another had stopped what they were doing. From the closest house and from one farther away, people hurried over to listen. Within a few minutes a crowd of people had gathered around Bree and Gna.

As Bree looked from one to another, she saw no one she knew. Bree only knew how helpless she was.

Again Gna stepped forward. For a moment Bree thought Gna would snatch the silver band from her neck. Grabbing hold, Bree clung to it as if it was a matter of life or death.

Around them, people muttered. It started first as a low word here or there. Then like an angry roar, their mutter rose in Bree's ears. Again she looked around for help. After what seemed like forever, she saw Mikkel on the edge of the crowd. He too looked angry.

Filled with panic, Bree again stepped back. With each step she took, Gna pressed toward her. Then to Bree's surprise, Mikkel stood next to her.

"What's wrong?" he asked quietly.

"Gna says this is her neckring."

"Is it?"

"Of course not!"

"But what is it? Something you made for me to sell?"

Bree shook her head. "Something I made for *me* to sell. To set Dev free."

Mikkel stared at her. "But our *ting* might do that when they vote."

"Maybe," Bree said. "Maybe not."

"So you stole hacksilver from me to set your brother free?"

"No! I didn't steal it from you!"

"But where—"

In that moment Bree remembered. Devin had told her to not tell anyone where she got the hacksilver. And now, that was exactly what Mikkel wanted to know.

"I can't tell you," Bree said.

"You can't tell me? But it's my silver, isn't it?"

As Mikkel looked around, Bree's gaze followed his. The crowd that surrounded them was growing by the minute. Many of them looked angry, and most, if not all of them, would take Gna's side. Bree felt sure of one thing. She needed to get out of there while she could.

Then with one quick movement Mikkel stepped in front of Bree and spoke directly into Gna's face. "Bree works for me. If you want the neckring, you must buy it."

In the same tone of voice he spoke to Bree. "Come."

With long strides and angry steps, Mikkel headed toward his father's longhouse.

By the time they reached the door, Mikkel's anger was so great that he looked like a thundercloud.

"Tell me," he said. "How can you use my silver and then not tell me where it came from?"

"It's not your silver," Bree said. "I know you won't believe me, but—"

In that moment Mikkel gave her the biggest surprise of all. "I *will* believe you, Bree," he said quietly. "Just tell me."

When Bree finished explaining, Mikkel asked one more question. "If the *ting* lets Devin go—if they let him use the ransom to free you, what will you do with the money from this neckring?

Not for anything would Bree tell him. "That's my secret," she said.

Then she realized how much Mikkel had done for her. In those terrible moments of danger and fear he had given his protection.

"A thousand thanks, Mikkel," Bree said. "I don't know what I would have done without you."

But Mikkel's face grew hard again. "There's just one thing," he said. "If I can't trust you to not do something so stupid, how can I trust you with walking in the mountains?"

Looking down, Bree drew a pattern in the snow with her boot. *Please God*, she prayed desperately. *I need to find Keely tonight.*

Mikkel's angry voice cut into her prayer. "No walking outside alone," he said. He pointed to the mountain wall on one side of the farm. "That's your boundary there." Turning to the fjord and the river, he said, "Your boundaries on those two sides."

"Please," Bree said as Mikkel turned the fourth direction. "I want to visit my brother Dev."

For a long moment Mikkel stared at her, as though trying to decide. Then he nodded. "You can go to the jail and no farther."

With a sinking heart, Bree nodded. At least she could see Dev. But Keely?

"If you don't obey, I'll tell Mamma that you have to stay in the house."

"Oh, no, Mikkel! I'll *die* if I'm stuck inside the house!" Always Bree had roamed the mountains. How could she possibly stay indoors every moment of the day or night? What would be worse?

Mikkel's cold smile told her he felt very glad he had found exactly the right punishment. "Remember that," he said. "Remember your boundaries."

The next time Bree saw Devin in the smithy, she told him how Mikkel had rescued her from Gna. Devin was so upset that he forgot to keep pounding his hammer. Instead, he stared at Bree with utter disbelief. "How did you ever manage to do something like that?"

"I wanted to help," Bree told him. "I turned your hacksilver into something really valuable. If the *ting* doesn't let you go, I'll have ransom to release you."

"There's just one thing you didn't think about."

In spite of her misery, Bree smiled. "More than one, probably."

"No one will ever believe the word of a slave."

"One slave, and one prisoner."

Devin dropped down on a bench. For several minutes he was silent, as though totally unable to speak. Bree stood nearby and stared at the packed earth floor just as long.

Finally Devin looked up. "Bree, don't you know the penalty for stealing? Don't you know what can happen to you?"

"I know." Bree's voice was small. "Stealing can be punished with death." She was tired of hearing about it, even more tired of thinking about it. "If I was found guilty I must pay back what I stole. I must also pay an extra amount to the person I dishonored by taking something from him."

"And if Mikkel says you took the silver from him—"

"He knows I didn't," Bree said.

"Does he?"

"Well—" Bree thought about it. "Maybe he does, and maybe he doesn't. He's got so many silver coins, maybe he really doesn't know. It could go either way."

"So it's up to Mikkel again, isn't it?"

The fear Bree felt went deep in her bones. "Even if he knows I didn't steal from him, can we trust him to do what's right?"

A strange look crossed Devin's face. "Trust. Remember? When Mikkel asked me to work for him, he asked me to trust him."

"And have you trusted him?" Bree asked.

Devin grinned for the first time that day. "Always with one eye open, watching him."

Suddenly Bree felt that he was her brother again. "Courage to win, Dev," she said.

"Courage to win, Bree. Jesus our Lord is Savior and King. We haven't asked Him for help."

Bowing their heads, they started to pray.

For the rest of the winter Bree obeyed Mikkel. For someone who had always been free to roam, staying within his boundaries felt like being in jail. Yet Bree knew one thing. If she stepped beyond the places Mikkel set for her, it would be even worse to not be able to go outside.

Then one afternoon the winds of spring lay warm upon the land. The next day a line of water appeared between the shore and the ice in the river. Not long after, the water tumbled around rocks in the stream, seeming happy to be set free.

On the day that ice and snow disappeared from the lower slopes, Bree saw Mikkel near the fjord. "I've obeyed you," she said to him. "I want to climb the mountains again."

Mikkel's steady gaze met hers. "Can I trust you to not run away?"

"I promised once," Bree said. "You can trust me." But inside she felt terrible about promising again.

Gradually the deep snows melted on the mountain-tops. When Mikkel's mother asked Bree to take Grandfather's axe to the boathouse, she set out with a light step. Walking along the sheer rock mountain at the side of the farm, Bree thought about Rika.

At first Bree hadn't been able to understand the quiet ways of these people of the North. Even when he was very angry with Mikkel, Sigurd had chosen his words carefully. By now Bree had lived on the fjord long enough to know that not everyone was careful with how they showed their feelings. When winter winds raged, keeping people inside for long periods of time, their tempers grew short. But Bree also understood something more— the depth of what these people thought and felt— though they didn't show it outwardly.

Their quiet ways did not mean they loved less. Nor did their quiet ways mean they couldn't express their thoughts well. Though many of the Norse words were still strange to Bree, she could hear the poetry in them. The promise of story. The song.

From watching Sigurd, Rika, and the grandparents, there was something Bree knew. *Their thoughts and their hearts go deep.*

Would there ever come a time when there would be no more Viking raids? A time when even Mikkel was honest and trustworthy?

Just then Bree looked down. A few days before, the

small stones on the slanted side of the boulder were pushed out of place. Now they were in order again.

No longer was there a letter K. The torch had been reshaped and another one added. Between the two torches there was something new. What was it?

At first Bree thought the stones outlined a bush without leaves. Then she realized the stones pictured an animal's head. A reindeer? Not a bush, but reindeer antlers?

As Bree remembered the reindeer pits on top of the mountains, she noticed something else. Between the sheer rock of the mountain and the water of the fjord was another message.

This one was made of larger stones. A round rock first, with a flat enough surface to set more stones on top. A second, third, and fourth stone carefully balanced to build a pillar. And then, at the very top—

If this was Keely, how had she managed to find such a rock? Rounded on one side, it had a definite wedge-shaped point on the other. Like an arrowhead, the rock pointed along the fjord.

Strange, Bree thought. *The one direction Rika never sent me. The one direction I didn't have time to take.*

Suddenly Bree laughed. Long ago Bree and Keely had played near the river that flowed past their home. Often they made up special games. This one was a secret between them. Their pointer rocks had marked hiding places when playing with Devin.

Keely, you're my invisible friend! But then Bree thought about it. *No, God is.*

Moments later, Bree heard Rika calling. After one last look, Bree turned away. *Tonight I'll be back!* There would even be a full moon to help her.

When her evening work was done, Bree hurried to the barn and pulled together the things she needed. An extra pair of wool stockings. The warm dress Rika had given her, a scarf, cloak, and mittens. The mountaintop would be cold at night, and Bree felt grateful for every piece of clothing she had.

Finally she put her wool blanket in a bag she could carry on her back. At the last minute Bree added a rope and the loose-fitting sealskin tunic and leggings she had made earlier. Food? She had saved bread from the evening meal.

With the full moon lighting her way, Bree crept out the door of the barn and through the animal pen. When she opened the gate in the stone fence, it squeaked, and Bree stopped and looked around. As she closed the gate, it squeaked again. Bree quickly slipped behind the line of trees at the base of the mountain.

Standing there, hidden by pines, Bree waited. All was quiet. Bree stayed behind the trees until she reached the boathouse. There she passed between the fjord and the sheer rock of the mountain. A short distance beyond she discovered a trail.

At first it was wide, but then it narrowed to pass beyond a large rock. When Bree heard a sound behind her, she whirled around. A shadow slipped out of sight.

Bree's heart pounded. *What was it? Or who?*

NINETEEN

THE REINDEER RUNS

Without moving, Bree stood there, looking back. Finally she decided she had imagined that some-one was there. Moving on, she picked up her pace. If there was anything she didn't want, it was the wrong per-son on this trail.

Sometimes the path lay close to the water. Other times it wound steeply upward to pass behind rock walls that dropped straight away to the fjord below.

A short distance farther on, Bree again whirled around. This time she was sure there was something behind her. When she saw Shadow, Bree groaned. The friendly dog was not known for being quiet. If he barked at the wrong time, he would give her away.

"Go home!" she said.

Shadow pricked his ears. Stopping, he looked back, then turned toward Bree, as though torn about what to do.

"Go home!" Bree commanded again. Instead, the dog sat down on his haunches. Cocking his head, he tipped it from side to side.

Bree started toward him. "Go home!"

Slowly the dog stood up. As though still not wanting to obey, he wagged his tail. Even in the moonlight, his eyes looked sad.

"I'm not going to change my mind," Bree told him. "Go home!"

After one more mournful look, Shadow turned around and started back to the farm.

Bree hurried on, but soon heard another noise behind her. This time it was Flurry who followed her. Bree couldn't believe what she was seeing. Who had opened the gate? And why was Flurry wearing her harness?

As though she and Shadow had talked about it, the horse seemed just as set on following her. It gave Bree a strange feeling. It was almost as if they wanted to keep her safe.

Bree pushed the thought away. She didn't care to think about danger. She only wanted to find Keely. But the way the animals acted made her uneasy.

When the mare reached her, Bree stroked her neck. Flurry's snuffle in her ear was full of satisfaction.

"All right, you can go with," Bree told her softly. "But be quiet." Bree set out again with Flurry following.

In the moonlight the fjord looked clear and cold, filled with a beauty Bree seldom had the opportunity to see. Her heart leaped as she looked at the mountains on the far side. She was on her way to see Keely!

Excitement raced in Bree's heart. Excitement warmed her insides and gave her courage for the unknown. *Keely will be there! I'll get to talk with my sister!*

With every step Bree looked forward to seeing the laughter in her sister's eyes. Keely's love for life spilled over to everyone around her.

Before long, clouds moved across the moon. As the night grew dark, Bree felt afraid of the steep, dangerous path. At first it had been easy to see the steep drops to the fjord. Now they were hidden from her. It was difficult enough when the moon shone brightly. How could she walk without light?

When Flurry nudged her aside, Bree caught hold of a strap in her harness and let the mare take the lead. Soon Bree felt glad that she had kept the sure-footed animal with her. In rocky stretches hidden by shadow it grew more and more difficult to walk. Some of the rocks still had slippery spots. Bree tried to take each step where Flurry did.

As Bree passed through the narrow places in the path, she stayed close to the mare's side. Now the mountain rose above her. Clouds still covered the moon and stars. Here the wind did not reach her, and Bree felt sheltered from the cold.

High above the fjord, she came to a cluster of farm buildings. Standing at a distance, she stopped and wondered what to do next. Then she saw it—another column of stacked stones, this one pointing to a trail up the mountain.

Her hand on Flurry's bridle, Bree whispered in her ear. "Shush now!" Without making a sound, they circled wide around the buildings. Beyond, they began climbing again.

Here there was snow and, with it, footprints of the right size for Keely. Sure that she would find her sister soon, Bree moved ahead, following the prints in the snow.

The mountain was steep here, but the trail was not dangerous. Usually Bree climbed with the skill of a mountain goat. Yet as she passed through a pine forest, it seemed that she walked forever. *Keely, what are you doing?* Bree wondered more than once. *Why are we meeting so far away?*

Bree hurried now in spite of the steep climb. She had no choice but to be back before daylight. Finally she reached the top of the mountain and it leveled out. Here on the heights the wind swept across the open ground, and with it came snow.

Leaning into the wind, Bree bent her head. The snow pricked her skin like tiny ice balls. Quickly she wrapped a scarf over her nose, forehead, and mouth. Yet with each step she felt the ice spitting against her eyes.

In some places snow lay in drifts between the rocks. In other places the earth was bare. Here there were few trees, and wind had swept away Keely's footprints.

Bree stared at the ground and saw nothing. Suddenly she felt the terror of it. *Am I here alone? Where is Keely?*

Then Bree reached out, touched Flurry's mane, and patted her strong neck. As if trying to offer comfort, Flurry stamped her hoof.

Unsure what to do, Bree stood there, looking around. As she waited, the wind blew the clouds away from the moon, and Bree saw a small hut. Built of stone, it lay under a rock overhang. Its door was so low that Bree would have to stoop to enter.

But then she remembered Flurry. Bree couldn't risk having the mare wander off. Opening the bag she carried on her back, Bree took out the rope and tied one end to a ring in Flurry's harness.

With the mare standing out of the wind, Bree took the loose end of the rope with her. When she crawled into the small hut, the hollow area beneath the overhang shut away the wind, snow, and cold. An opening in the outer wall gave Bree the ability to look out.

Bree felt sure it was a shelter used by hunters. For a moment she sank down, breathed deep, and rested. But then she grew sleepy and knew how deadly that might be.

Going outside again, Bree coiled the rope and pushed it under a strap in Flurry's harness. "Keely! Keely!" Bree called. "Where are you?"

The wind caught her voice and flung it back. Ke-e-e-e-ly! Ke-e-e-ely!

Over and over Bree called, but the wind snatched away the sound. Ke-e-e-e-ly!

Afraid to leave the hut, afraid she would lose her bearings and become stranded, Bree stood still. In that white wasteland was there no tree, no brush, no outcropping of rock? Nothing to help her find her way back?

Then Bree saw that off to her right was one lone tree. Her gaze on that tree, Bree caught Flurry's bridle and set out across the ground filled with blowing snow. Partway there, Bree remembered Rika's words. *Reindeer runs.*

Deep inside, Bree sensed the warning. *Open pits.* Pits to catch the reindeer as they ran across the mountaintops. Pits so deep that even a reindeer could not leap back out.

Bree's shiver had nothing to do with cold. When she found a branch, she used it to feel the ground in front of her. With one hand still on Flurry's bridle and her other hand holding the stick, Bree moved forward slowly.

Before each step she tested the ground with the stick. With every place Bree set her foot, she watched to see if Flurry walked there first. Again and again Bree called out, "Keely! Where are you?"

Bree had almost reached the tree when she heard a voice. "Bree! Help me!"

The voice sounded so far away that Bree moved quickly, forgetting to feel the ground. Just in time, she tapped the stick. The ground had vanished.

In that instant Flurry backed away, pulling Bree with her. Terror in her heart, Bree dropped to her knees. When she reached out, she felt the edge of a hole. The edge of nothing.

"Keely!" Bree called. "Where are you?"

"In a hole." Keely's voice was closer now, but eerie sounding.

From where Bree knelt, afraid to move, she looked down into a pit lined with stones. In the moonlight, she could see that the sides of the long, narrow pit fell away to nothing. Beyond Bree, the pit was covered with brush and larger branches that hid the opening.

"Keely! Is it really you?"

A small voice rose from the darkness. "It's really me."

Bree's heart thumped. From Devin's description this wasn't what she expected. She had expected arms thrown around her. One of Keely's famous hugs.

And then Bree knew. "Are you hurt?"

"I'm hurt bad."

"Your head?" Bree asked. "Your arms? Your back?"

"My right foot. I can climb out of most anything, but these sides are straight up and down."

"Where are you?"

"Move along the side," Keely said.

"Keep talking," Bree told her. On her hands and knees Bree crawled around outside the pit, moving carefully past the brush that hid the opening. At last she knelt over the spot where she heard Keely best. It was still too dark to see her sister.

"I'm cold, Bree. Really cold."

Quickly Bree pushed branches aside and opened the bag she carried on her back. The sealskin tunic and leggings spilled out. Bree dropped the tunic down, then ripped the bottom of the right leg in case Keely's foot was swollen. "Can you pull these on over your clothes?"

Bree's warm blanket was next in the bag, but then she remembered the rope tied to a ring in Flurry's harness. Keely was light and climbed well most of the time.

With stiff fingers Bree made a loop in the free end of the rope. "Grab hold," she called as she threw it down to her sister. "Can you get to the end of the pit and walk up the wall?"

Flurry planted her feet, ready to help, but it was more difficult than it sounded. When Keely fell back, Bree knew she had hurt herself more than she wanted to admit.

Again Bree called down. "When we pull up, push your good foot against the wall of the pit. Lean back."

Again Keely clung to the rope. With one foot bouncing against the wall, she let Flurry pull her higher and higher. At last Bree caught hold of Keely's arm and helped her the rest of the way.

When they both knelt a safe distance from the pit, they threw their arms around each other. Bree had forgotten what it meant to feel her sister's hug. Suddenly both of them were sobbing.

Keely pulled back first to look at her older sister. "If Daddy and Mam could see us now!"

Bree giggled with her. "Hugging instead of fighting!"

Again they hugged, and then Bree helped Keely onto Flurry's back. When they reached the shelter for hunters, their words tumbled out.

For all this time Keely had lived on the farm that Bree had passed on her way up the mountain. Because she too slept in a barn, she was able to creep out at night and often did.

What could they do, now that they were together?

"I brought food," Keely said. "Let's keep going over the mountains."

But Bree had seen her sister flinch each time she tried to put weight on her foot. It was surprising that Keely hadn't hurt herself more.

"We can't," Bree said.

"Yes, we can. You can creep down and get Dev—"

Through the moonlight that reached into the shelter, Bree saw Keely's face. Light seemed to fill even her eyes.

"Oh, Bree, I heard Dev playing the pipes. The lullaby Mam used to sing to us. I saw him come in, just like I saw you come in. First you, then my brother—"

Keely's face crumpled with just the thought of it. "After six years—"

"Keely, are you all right?" Bree asked. "Really, really all right?"

Keely blinked away her tears. "Daddy and Mam—they prayed for me, didn't they?"

Bree nodded. "We all prayed for you. Adam, and Cara, and Jen prayed for you, too."

"Cara? Jen?"

And then Bree knew—really knew—what Keely had lost. *Six years.* Bree had forgotten how long six years would be for her sister.

"You don't know, do you?" Bree asked gently. "Your brother Adam is seven now, and you have two new sisters, Cara and Jen. And didn't you wonder if we'd ever see each other again?"

"Think about it," Keely said. "Even when I was a little girl—a girl no more than this high—" She held out her hand. "Brother Cronan talked about miracles. It's a miracle, isn't it, that we've found each other?"

Bree agreed. "A miracle, all right. Someone must have told Mikkel about the monastery."

"Well, let's ask God for another miracle—that we get away."

Bree had no problem with that prayer. But when Keely wanted to leave in the next moment, Bree had to hold her back. "We'll escape," she promised. "But we have to plan it right."

"If they know we're sisters, they'll keep us apart," Keely said. "They won't give us a chance to escape."

"Is that why you kept hiding from me?" Bree asked. "So we wouldn't meet in the open?"

Keely nodded. "During the winter they caught me sneaking out at night. They set a watch on me."

"But before that, you came at night," Bree said. "Why didn't you find me then?"

"I couldn't come every night, and the dogs always barked. I knew they'd wake everyone up. But someone walks outside the house where you live."

Bree stared at her. "And around the barn?" Often Bree had wondered if she heard footsteps. "Who is it?"

"A man or older boy. I couldn't get close enough to tell. He paces, going back and forth like something is wrong."

TWENTY

ON TRIAL

Keely leaned forward. "Bree, is there some way we can creep down and rescue Dev?"

This was the choice Bree dreaded. "I needed to make a trade," she said. "I needed freedom to search for you. But I had to promise I would not run away."

To Bree's surprise Keely understood. The sister who had always darted this way and that, flitting like an elf between trees, put it straight.

"You're right, Bree. You have to keep a promise."

That settled it. From then on, they talked about ways to meet again and their hope for all three of them to be free.

When they went outside again, Bree helped Keely

onto Flurry's back. As though knowing she carried a precious load, the mare stepped carefully across the mountaintop and down the trail. As daylight crept upon the fjord, Bree left Keely as close as possible to the farm where she lived.

With tears in their eyes, they hugged each other goodbye. "Don't forget our secret signal," Keely said, reminding Bree to watch for pointer rocks. They would meet halfway between the two farms on the trail next to the fjord.

"Three nights from now," Keely told her. Then, using Bree's stick, she limped away.

When Bree was safely on the trail again, she stopped at a high point and looked across the deep blue waters of the fjord. A dusting of snow still lay on the top of the mountains. Off to Bree's left the spray of a waterfall tumbled down a steep slope. As Bree watched the falling water, all that had happened to her seemed to fit into place.

She, Dev, and Keely had walked through hard days. No doubt there were more hard days to come. But now as Bree took a deep breath, the weight of all she had carried fell away. *Lord, You have set my heart free!*

For a time Bree stood there, unable to move on. Then she remembered. At the farm Mikkel would miss Flurry first. Then he'd miss her. She could be accused of stealing the horse.

At the beginning of the trail along the fjord, Bree slapped the mare's rump. "Go on home." Flurry turned her head, looked at Bree, then obeyed.

Walking quickly in the growing light, Bree followed her. This time the song she hummed was not for Grandmother or for Molly the cow. By now Bree knew it wasn't her voice that counted most, but her grateful heart.

As she left the trail and passed the boathouse, Mikkel came outside. "You're back," he said.

"Yes, I'm back," Bree answered.

"You could have kept going over the mountains. Why didn't you?"

More than anything in her life Bree had wanted to rescue Dev and keep going. Couldn't they somehow have managed? Regret filled Bree at the thought of it.

But then she met Mikkel's gaze. "Because I promised."

"You didn't think about breaking that promise?"

Bree smiled. "Of course. With all my heart I wanted to break that promise."

"I never would have seen you again."

Bree heard the strangeness in Mikkel's voice, then the wonder that she had stayed.

"Why?" Mikkel's question shot out like an arrow. "Why did you come back?"

Bree thought about it. There on the mountain what had she known? Truth could set Mikkel free. If she broke her promise to not run away, what would happen to him?

Then Bree remembered the reason that Keely also understood. "I knew that if I broke a promise, you would think that all the other things I've said are not true."

Once more Bree set out. She had nearly reached the barn when she saw Cort standing next to the stone fence. When Bree tried to slip past him, he called to her.

"You came back," Cort said, as Mikkel had.

Bree stopped. When she looked at this brother who always seemed on the edge of the family, she knew. "Why do you walk outside at night?"

Cort's face showed his surprise. At first it seemed he would not answer, but then he said, "I can't sleep, trying to figure things out. I never thought I'd have to take Ivar's place. That was bad enough. With my father sick, it's even worse. How can I do things the way he would do them? How can I be like him?"

"You don't have to be like either of them," Bree said. "Just take care of the land and the people."

"But how can I care for others when I don't even like my own brother? How can I be fair if I can't be fair with him? Mikkel succeeds at everything he does."

"Not quite," Bree said. It couldn't be called success to steal from his father's friend. But she couldn't say that to Mikkel's brother.

"You came here as a slave, but you've been kind to us. How do you do it?"

Bree knew she hadn't done it by herself. But would

Cort understand that? "I started to love Grandmother," she said. "I had to choose to forgive."

Then Bree remembered the night Molly the cow talked. "I had to stop feeling sorry for myself and try to help others."

When Cort grinned as though saying *yes*, it was the first time Bree saw him smile. "You're the one who let the mare out," she said.

"I saw you leave. I wanted you to be free, but I wanted you to be safe."

"Thank you," Bree said. "Flurry saved my life."

As she opened the gate and started through the pen to the barn, she saw Mikkel standing between the pines as if listening.

Then the last of the ice and snow melted, and spring was full upon the land. Eagles soared above the mountains. Seals swam in the fjord but disappeared whenever a boat came close. One morning Bree stood in the doorway of the longhouse and heard the call of a bird she knew well. *Cuckoo! Cuckoo! Cuckoo!*

Bree stared at the sheer rock that rose straight up along the edge of the farm. The call came from the left side of the mountain. As Bree watched, the bird flew to the right side. As it perched there, calling out its cuckoo, it reminded Bree of home.

That afternoon Bree found Devin working alone. None of the children who loved to hear his stories were there. No one lingered outside the smithy.

"We can talk," Bree said.

"So begin," Dev told her. He was building up muscles from his work as a blacksmith and was wise enough to keep pounding his hammer while they talked.

Bree found a small stool and pulled it close enough to talk without being heard. To her surprise, Dev admitted his discouragement.

"When the assembly of freemen meets, who will speak for me?" he asked.

"Sigurd would have defended you," Bree said.

"He would speak against Mikkel? How can he be just when his own son would lose the ransom money?"

Bree had thought about that. "It's because he loves his son that Sigurd would be fair. He doesn't want Mikkel to get by with something he shouldn't."

Devin sighed. "Well, whatever Sigurd might do, I guess it doesn't count. With leprosy he can't do anything."

As Bree stood up to go, her brother stopped her. "Do you know what bothers me most? Sometimes I really like Mikkel. If things were different, we could be good friends—like brothers even. But the Viking raid, the coins he stole—Mikkel doesn't know I know about the coins, but they keep coming between us."

"I know," Bree said. The same things upset her.

"It's like he's a slave to greed," Devin said.

Bree remembered Sigurd's words on her first day in Aurland. "That's what his father said. He told Mikkel, 'Unless you find a way to set your actions right, you'll be a slave to what you have done.'"

Devin stared at Bree. "No wonder you think that Sigurd is a wise and just man."

"Mikkel could be, too."

Her brother grinned. "But how will he ever manage to change?"

Each time Bree brought food to Sigurd she knocked on a small door similar to the one in the jail. The opening was just big enough for passing food and water.

Today Mikkel's father was standing in the doorway, looking across the field to the river and the fjord. Like Devin, Sigurd seemed to be growing more discouraged with each day.

"Tomorrow my friends will come from far and near," he said as he spoke about the assembly of freemen. "They'll talk together and make wise choices, and I will not be there."

As Sigurd took his plate from Bree, he asked, "Your brother Devin? How is he doing?"

"He's a good blacksmith," she said. "He's lost count of the rivets he's made for Mikkel."

Sigurd looked pleased, but then asked, "Who will speak for him at the *ting?*"

Yes, who? Bree wondered. *Who will take Devin's side?*

"I don't know," she said. Forcing back her tears, Bree turned away. Was there anyone else as wise as Sigurd and trusted enough for people to listen?

But then Sigurd asked her about Naaman the leper. "I have built great ships and sailed to far places. How would I get to the Jordan River?"

"You don't have to go there," Bree said. "When Jesus was here on earth, He healed lepers. You can go to Him."

"This Jesus," Sigurd said. "We have many gods, but none by that name. Is He another god?"

"No," Bree said. "He's the only true God, the one who died on a cross for you."

"We have a god like that. He hung upside down in a tree to gain knowledge. Is your god also cruel?"

Bree shook her head. "Jesus hung, head up, with a sign that said, 'This is Jesus, King of the Jews.' But He did it because He loves us. Jesus is the one to ask for help."

"What kind of help?"

"With everything," Bree said. "Even if you don't get better—even if your leprosy doesn't go away—it would help you to know Him. He would comfort you when you're alone, away from your family."

For a time Sigurd stood there, silent, but seeming to think it through. Finally he spoke. "This Jesus. Would

He want to help me when I have never done anything for Him?"

"Oh, yes!" Bree exclaimed. "That's how He is. If He was here on earth, He would reach out His hand and touch you."

"But He's not here."

"Not that we can see. But He tells us to just come to Him. The way you would talk with one of your friends."

Again Sigurd stood there without speaking. His thoughtful look reminded Bree of the day that Mikkel brought home a ship filled with slaves. This wise man was so close to understanding how Jesus could set him free. But how could she ever explain?

Then Bree knew. Sigurd's words had stayed with her all these months. When she was discouraged they had brought comfort and hope.

"Do you remember what you said to Mikkel on my first day here?" she asked. "You told him, 'You're a slave to whatever you serve.'"

When Sigurd nodded, Bree again saw pain in his eyes. "Someday there will not be slavery in my country. I want Mikkel to be a merchant, not a raider. And you, Bree. You should not be a slave."

"I'm not a slave," Bree said. In that moment she realized she was no longer afraid of catching leprosy. Instead, she only felt glad that she could talk to Sigurd in this way.

"I'm more free than Mikkel." She began to tell Sigurd about it.

"And this Jesus," he finally asked. "He really would help me when I've never done anything for Him?"

"He would help you in the way He knows is best for you."

"I must think," Sigurd said, turning back into the small building. "I must consider."

As Bree watched, he closed the door behind him.

When Bree looked outside the next morning, boats of all kinds were already streaming into the fjord. Some were simple boats for bringing hay from the mountain pastures. Others were proud Viking longships. By mid-morning every piece of shore had been taken up. People were also walking in from the mountains.

Soon tents sprang up wherever there was room. The only area left open was part of the large field behind the chieftain's house. There children played on the green meadow. Young men competed in archery, and women set out food.

As Bree watched, she saw that people followed a certain order. Whether eating, talking, or playing games, everyone left an opening around the rounded earth mound where the lawspeaker would stand.

When it came time for the meeting of freemen to

begin, people sat down on the grassy slopes, facing that mound. Like sand on the seashore, they spread across the land between the Aurland River and the mountain.

At the back of the crowd Bree stood beside her brother. His two guards stood on the other side behind Devin. Neither guard had seen fit to bind his hands, perhaps because he had worked among them as a blacksmith. But Bree noticed their watchful eyes.

As she looked around, Bree saw a slender girl with sandy colored hair, a dusting of freckles across her nose, and dark brown eyes just like their mother's. Keely's long braid bounced whenever she moved. Sunlight danced in her eyes and caught the funny tuft of hair on top of her head.

Someone had cut a branch with a Y-shaped notch to help Keely walk. Though she used it for support now and then, there was nothing else in Keely that leaned. When she grinned at Bree, it was the grin she wore when she was up to something—often a trick on Bree or Dev. But when Bree started her way, Keely shook her head.

She was still being wise, acting as if she did not know either Bree or Dev. With Gna lurking around, Bree felt glad.

Keely and Lil had found each other. Watching them, Bree knew they could be lifelong friends. But where would they live? If Bree had anything to say about it, it would be Ireland.

Near the lawspeaker's mound, Mikkel sat on the ground beside his brother Cort. When she saw them talking, Bree felt surprised, then upset. Why would they be together unless they had reached an agreement? And wouldn't any agreement be against Dev?

Bree sighed and tried to ignore the tight knot in her stomach. The two brothers had power. Were they not the chieftain's sons? And Mikkel had given work to many men. Who would vote against him? Who would say that Mikkel should not have the money? And who would say that a slave captured on a raid to Ireland should be allowed to go free?

On the other hand, if they freed Devin, they might also free her. The possibility was so exciting that Bree could barely stand there. But then the fear that it might never happen washed over her like a wave in the stormy North Sea.

One freeman after another stood to speak. Then came the most persuasive of all.

"When we trap the fox that roam our mountains we set the trap carefully," he said. "But the hunter does not choose which fox will be caught. It is the fox himself that decides whether he will be caught. He chooses whether to enter the trap in search of the bait."

Throughout the audience men grinned at each other. Without doubt, they knew what the speaker was saying.

"On our raid to Ireland the boy of whom we speak

became a prisoner. Out of the kindness of his heart, Mikkel set him free to return home. But then that prisoner, of his own free will, walked back into the trap."

"Do we need to be kind again? What if our enemies hear of it? Is it not important that they fear us? That they know how strong we are? Do we not have peace because they are afraid of us?"

From all over the crowd cheers broke out. One man after another waved his arms in the air, agreeing with the speaker. Bree felt a coldness in her hands, then in her heart. Reaching out, she took her brother's hand. It felt just as cold as her own. As though trying to offer comfort, Devin squeezed her hand, then let it go.

Then as Bree looked around, she saw Hauk standing at the side of the crowd. His face was serious, his eyes as piercing as always. But then Hauk smiled. *Smiled?*

The man with Hauk had his back toward Bree. When he turned, Bree saw his face. *Sigurd? Mikkel's father? Could it possibly be?*

As Sigurd started forward through the crowd, he walked like a warrior with shoulders back and head high. His gray-white hair and beard were trimmed close, and his face seemed filled with light. When he passed between the people in one row, then another, they looked his way. Suddenly they realized who he was.

All through the crowd, people stood up, grabbed the

arm of a person nearby. Like a wave rolling in from the sea, excited voices rose as one person told another.

Following close behind Sigurd, Hauk walked as though bearing armor for a king. When the two men reached the open area next to the lawspeaker's mound, they bowed before him. The crowd fell silent.

Hauk spoke first. "Respected Lawspeaker, I have come to verify the health of our honorable chieftain, Sigurd. He is no longer unclean. He is full of good health!"

Clasping Sigurd's hand, Hauk held it high. The crowd broke into a cheer. Had God really done a miracle? Even though Bree knew He could do anything He wanted, she still found it hard to believe.

Then Bree looked at Devin, and Devin looked at Bree. When Devin grinned he stood with head back, looking up. He looked up for a long time.

SLAVE OR FREE?

When everyone quieted down, Sigurd bowed toward the lawspeaker, then faced the crowd.

"Good people of the Aurland Fjord," he began. Turning from one side of the audience to the other, Sigurd continued by greeting those from other fjords and mountains near and far.

As Sigurd spoke, Bree was surprised at the strength in his voice. From where she stood near the back, she could hear every word.

"There are those who say we do not have to show kindness. But what if no kindness was shown to us? We are talking about a ransom to set free a person who has been kind to us."

Suddenly people turned and looked toward the back, seeking Bree out. Their notice of her made Bree uncomfortable. Trying to hide her feelings, she set her gaze on the mountain behind where Sigurd stood. Today the sun reached into the valley from that direction.

As Sigurd went on, even the small children were silent, listening. "Today we speak about something much bigger than one person, two, three, or four. We speak about something that goes far beyond the Aurland Fjord."

Holding out his hand, Sigurd motioned toward the mountains in front of him, behind, to his left, and to his right. "Something even bigger than our mountains. Something that lives after us, that makes us who we are."

"Do we face a small decision or a large one? Do we want a decision that says we are small people or big of heart? Do we want a decision that says we are just and fair?

"In the history of our world there have been Norwegians of other times and places who have faced such a choice. In the future there will be people in other lands who ask themselves this question. We cannot choose for them, only for ourselves. Can a person who brings ransom for another be taken as a prisoner? Can that person be enslaved himself? Put in jail and left there? If he can, then who among us will rescue a friend or a neighbor who needs help?"

This time Devin stretched out his hand to Bree. Clasping hers, Devin stood there, motionless and watchful. Shoulders back, head high, he waited.

When Sigurd sat down, the lawspeaker called for a vote. "Freemen of the mountains and fjords, you gather here to make wise and just decisions. First, should the young man known as Devin O'Toole of Ireland be set free?"

In the silence that followed, one freeman after another raised his hand. Fingers balled in a fist, they held their arms outstretched toward the lawspeaker. Then somewhere near the front a cry began. "Yes, yes, yes!"

Turning, the lawspeaker looked from one upheld arm to another. When the lawspeaker nodded, they lowered their arms. Hardly daring to breathe, Bree stole a look at Devin.

The lawspeaker waited for silence, then spoke again. "The second choice is this. Should the ransom money be returned to the young man who came to set his sister free?"

Watching and waiting, Bree caught her breath. Everyone knew it was Mikkel, the chieftain's own son, who would lose. Return the money to a foreigner? An Irishman? So he could use that money to set free an Irish slave?

Down near the lawspeaker's mound, a freeman raised his hand. With a balled fist, he extended his arm toward the lawspeaker. Nearby, another freeman raised his arm. To the left and to the right, one arm after another went up.

Again the lawspeaker looked from one upheld arm to

another. Then it seemed that every freeman in that great crowd lifted his arm toward the speaker.

Suddenly one man stood up. Another joined him. Like a wave rolling in from the sea it swept from the river side of that great assembly toward the mountain. One person after another rose to his feet, as though proud to be part of something so good.

Tears in her eyes, Bree squeezed her brother's hand. Then Keely was there, standing between them, clasping their hands. The funny tuft of hair on top of her head stood up. Her long braid swung down her back. When she offered her lopsided grin, she too was weeping.

Then the lawspeaker called Mikkel, Devin, and Bree forward. Picking up the bag of ransom money, the lawspeaker gave it to Devin.

As Devin handed the money to Mikkel, he spoke in a solemn voice. "I pay this to you, Mikkel, in order to set free my sister Briana."

Free!

For one moment Bree stood there, before the lawspeaker and the freemen who had given respect to her and Devin. For one moment Bree felt the miracle of it. *Free!*

Then Mikkel spoke. "I accept this ransom from you, Devin O'Toole, for the freeing of your sister Briana."

When Mikkel turned to Bree, he lowered his voice. "I am sorry to see you go." As tears welled up in his eyes,

Mikkel stopped, swallowed hard, and went on. "But I am glad you will be free."

Free! Again Bree felt the miracle of it. Standing there, she wanted to feel that moment forever.

But then as Mikkel brushed a hand across his eyes, Bree looked up at the lawspeaker. "I would like to give my freedom to my sister Keely."

Facing the crowd, Bree motioned to Keely. As she started forward, a murmur went from one person to the next.

Mikkel stared at Bree. "This is your sister? You want to give your freedom away?"

Bree nodded, then spoke quietly to the lawspeaker. "And I would like to give this as ransom for an eight-year-old girl. Would it be enough?"

Taking the neckring she had hidden beneath her cloak, Bree handed it to the lawspeaker. He in turn gave it to another man.

As they talked between them, Bree looked back to Lil. The eight-year-old was doing her best to look happy for Keely. But Bree knew Lil too well. She was really doing her best to not cry.

Then the lawspeaker spoke to Bree. "The answer is yes," he said. "And it would pay for her passage home." By vote of the assembly, both Keely and Lil were set free.

When Devin, Bree, Keely, and Lil walked to the back of the crowd, they went down to the fjord. Keely was still stunned by what had happened. "For a minute I thought you both would leave me—"

"No, no!" Bree exclaimed. "Dev and I could never leave you."

"But how can we leave *you?*"

"Mam and Daddy haven't seen you for six years. You should be the one to go."

"You're sure? You're making the right choice?"

Suddenly Bree felt as if Keely was the older sister. "I'm sure," Bree answered. "I want you to go home with Devin."

For another moment Keely stood there, as though still unable to believe what had happened. Then one tear slid down her cheek. As that tear reached her chin, she started sobbing as if she suddenly felt all the loneliness she had known for years.

When Bree opened her arms, Keely walked into them. "Oh, Bree!" she said at last when she could finally speak. "I never thought I'd be free again. I never thought I'd see you or Dev or Mam or Daddy or Adam again."

"Don't forget your two new sisters," Bree said softly.

Keely's smile was like sunlight coming through clouds. "It's hard to imagine, isn't it? I can't even think what it will be like to see them when I didn't know they were there."

As Bree turned to her eight-year-old friend, Lil could barely speak. "I'll never forget you, Bree," Lil said when she could thank her. "Thanks for being my big sister."

But Devin also asked Bree, "Are you sure about this?"

Bree blinked her tears away. "I'm sure about this." *I ache inside, but I'm sure.* "I thought about it all winter long."

Then Mikkel was there, looking from one to the other. "Keely is going home? And Lil? And you, Devin? Take Keely and Lil to Ireland, and then come back."

"No, Dev," Bree said quickly. "You must not come back!" She wasn't willing to take a chance on what might happen.

But her brother's steady gaze met hers. Both of them knew that Bree still needed a way to get home.

"Come back and be my storyteller," Mikkel said.

"I'm Irish," Devin told him. "I'm not like your poets. I don't think that way."

"No matter!" Mikkel answered. "Storytelling is in your bones. If you and Bree go with me on one voyage, I'll set her free when we return home."

Free! Bree thought. The word hung in the air between them.

Always she had been free to roam the mountains that she loved. Always she had been free to learn and grow and wonder what lay beyond the Irish Sea. But Mikkel's world was even bigger. Not only had he dreamed about sailing to faraway places, he had done it. And now he had built a new ship that would probably go even farther.

If Mikkel did explore distant seas, where would he

sail? What lands would he see? What would it mean if she and Dev went with him?

But Devin still stood there, waiting, as though trying to decide. Mikkel still faced him. And Mikkel spoke again.

"Be my storyteller," he said. "But most of all, be my friend."

Devin looked Mikkel straight in the eye. "One voyage, and you will set my sister free," Devin said. "I will be your storyteller. And I will be your friend."

When Mikkel stretched out his hand, they shook on it.

Turning, Bree looked at the fjord. The high mountain with the waterfall that spilled over the top lay before her. Beyond the Aurland Fjord, beyond the long waterway that led to the western islands and the sea—what lay beyond?

After seeing the world, she would really be free? She could go home?

Her heart filled with gladness, Bree smiled.

ACKNOWLEDGMENTS

When we meet someone we often ask, "Where do you live?" or "Where are you from?" It's an easy way to get acquainted. The places we know best are fun to talk about. They're also an important part of who we are.

But if you live in a small town or a farming community, think about what it would be like to have 2,800 people leave your area. That's what happened between 1840 and 1920 in Aurland, the area in Norway used as a setting in this novel. Because of that emigration, there are now countless Americans who trace their ancestry to the Aurland Fjord.

I am especially indebted to Anders Ohnstad, historian,

author, and retired high school teacher, who helped me with his articles and books, his in-depth knowledge, his thoughtful understanding of people and events, and his warm Norwegian welcome.

Thank you, Anders, for your personal faith and courage and for the long talks in which you made the history of the Aurland area come alive. Thank you for the insights that helped me understand who Mikkel's father, Sigurd, should be. When I knew that, I also understood who Mikkel might be in this and earlier novels, and who he might become in the future.

Ingvar Vikesland not only helped me when I visited Aurland, but also gave ongoing assistance with follow-up questions. He has provided a patient and valuable link for all that I needed to know. Teacher and headmaster, now principal at the Local History Center in Aurland, Ingvar is a gifted communicator and able guide. He has been exceedingly helpful, and I cannot say *tusen takk* enough!

My gratitude to Åsmund Ohnstad, high school teacher, author, and editor of *Among the Fjords and Mountains: A summary of Aurland's history* (Aurland Historical Association, 1994). Thanks to all the authors of this excellent book and to Frazier LaForce, a teacher and local cultural consultant.

The Local History Center in Aurland houses a fine museum. Nearby is the beautiful Vangen Church. Built in the early Gothic style, the cornerstone for this church was laid in 1202. The Otternes Museum located farther along the Aurland Fjord is also of great interest.

If you're acquainted with Norwegian fjords, you'll know that most of them do not freeze in cold weather. However, the inner part of a fjord may freeze. As an arm of the Sognefjord, the Aurland Fjord is about 130 miles in from the Norwegian Sea. Within the memory of people who live in the area, the fjord, the Aurland River, and a spring used for drinking water usually froze over in winter.

Today we understand the importance of the Vikings who set foot on North American soil approximately 500 years before Columbus. But do we also understand their influence on our American legal system? Our right to hold a trial, to decide who is innocent or guilty, and our right to vote? In his book *Encyclopaedia of the Viking Age*, John Haywood writes about Findan, an Irishman who was sent to ransom his sister. Findan was clapped in irons while his sister's captors decided what to do with him. The *ting* scene in this novel is based on a Viking decision that it is not ethical to kidnap people who come to pay ransom.

The disease called leprosy in the Bible is also called Hansen's disease because of the work of G. Armauer Hansen, a physician in Bergen, Norway. In 1874, he discovered the bacillus (rod-shaped bacterium) that causes leprosy.

In addition to the people already named I would like to thank the following:

In Norway:

The Viking Ship Museum, Oslo; the Bergen Maritime Museum, Bergen, especially for its exhibit showing the construction of a Viking ship; Captain Bjørn Ols'en, retired, volunteer, for his helpful explanations; Arne Loitegard and Otto Langmoen.

In Northern Ireland:

Elaine Roub, faithful encourager, for walking the seashores and mountains with me.

In the Republic of Ireland:

Christopher Stacey, Mountain Leader, Footfalls Walking Holidays, County Wicklow, www.walkinghiking ireland.com; Dr. Felicity Devlin, Education Officer, Education and Outreach Department, National Museum of Ireland, Dublin.

In the United States:

Millie Ohnstad, heritage tour leader and genealogical editor of *Aurland Newsletter, Past and Present.* Many descendants of Aurland residents return for a visit under her leadership. My gratitude, Millie, for your heartwarming encouragement, photos, maps, and practical help, and to you, Ann Forsman, for editing the newsletter, www. aurlandnewsletter.com.

Dr Bjorn Hurlen, Lake Region Family Chiropractic Clinic and former resident of Bergen; Sons of Norway for the resources at their Minneapolis headquarters and their *Viking* Magazine; LaDonn Kjersti-Mae Jonsen, Special Events and Culture Specialist, Sons of Norway; Thomas Pedersen, Viking resource person; Dennis Rusinko and other members of the Viking Age Club; Dr. Arne Brekke, president, Brekke Tours & Travel.

Vikings: The North Atlantic Saga exhibit, organized by the Smithsonian's National Museum of Natural History, Washington, D.C., exhibited at the Science Museum of Minnesota, St. Paul.

Vassilena Ouzounova, for the excellent article she wrote as a high school student and her understanding that self-respect is more important than self-esteem.

Vicki Palmquist, founder, Children's Literature Network; Mary Ekola, fabric artist; Kathleen Lofquist, for her helpful insights; Stan and Jocelyn Anderson and Neil and Ruth Sorum, Sorum Fjord Horse Farm, for their great help with Fjord horses.

Special resource people—Michael, Lizabeth, Lincoln, and Davika Towers; David and Anne Gran; Dee and Chuck Brown; Robert Elmer; Dr. Michael Foss; Karen Odegard; Judy Werness; Diane Cudo; Judy Carter; Sue and Steve Davidson; my Thursday morning group, and longtime praying friends.

My agent, Lee Hough and Alive Communications; Ron Klug, wise encourager and friend; Barbara LeVan Fisher for her cover design and logo; Greg Call for his cover illustration and inside art.

My supportive editors—Michele Straubel, Amy Schmidt, Cessandra Dillon, Pam Pugh; author relations manager Amy Peterson; publicity coordinator Lori Wenzinger; typesetter Carolyn McDaniel; and the entire Moody team.

Our neighbors, friends, and family. You are so numerous that I cannot begin to name all of you. Your prayers and practical help made an incredible difference at a crucial time. Thank you!

My husband, Roy. Thanks for being a man of gentle strength. Thanks for your caring heart. And thanks for being my favorite Norwegian Viking.

Most of all, my gratitude to my Lord, who is always faithful, whether the wind blows cold or the wind blows fair.

In addition to the Aurland book already mentioned, I have found the following books and Web sites especially helpful:

Fitzhugh, William W. and Elisabeth I. Ward, editors, *Vikings: The North Atlantic Saga*, Smithsonian Institution Press, Washington and London, in association with the National Museum of Natural History, ©2000 by the Smithsonian Institution.

Haywood, John, *Encyclopaedia of the Viking Age*, Thames and Hudson, Inc., New York, N.Y., ©2000.

Joyce, P. W., *A Social History of Ancient Ireland*, vols. 1 & 2, originally published 1903, republished in the U.S., Kansas City, Mo: Irish Genealogical Foundation, 1997.

Konstam, Angus, *Historical Atlas of the Viking World*, Checkmark Books, New York, N.Y., ©2002 by Thalamus Publishing.

The Viking Network website, sponsored by The Nordic Council of Ministers, http://viking.no.

The Norwegian Fjord Horse Registry, http://www.nfhr.com

Sorum Fjord Horse Farm website, http://www.sorumfjordfarm.com

Viking Quest Series
Books 1 & 2

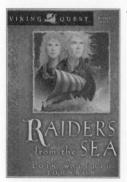

ISBN: 0-8024-3112-7

Raiders from the Sea

In one harrowing day, Viking raiders capture Bree and her brother Devin and take them from their home in Ireland. After the young Viking leader Mikkel sets Devin free on the Irish coast far from home, Bree and Devin embark on separate journeys to courage. You will be captivated by the unfolding drama as Bree sails to Norway on the Viking ship and Devin travels the dangerous road home. They both must trust their all-powerful God in the midst of difficult situations.

ISBN: 0-8024-3113-5

Mystery of the Silver Coins

In this second installment of the Viking Quest series, Bree finds herself in a physical and spiritual battle for survival in the homeland of her Viking captors.

Bree must face her unwillingness to forgive the Vikings, and Mikkel, the Viking leader who captured Bree, begins to wonder: Is the god of these Irish Christians really more powerful than our own Viking gods?

MOODY
PUBLISHERS

THE NAME YOU CAN TRUST.

1-800-678-6928 www.MoodyPublishers.com

THE INVISIBLE FRIEND TEAM

ACQUIRING EDITOR
Michele Straubel

COPY EDITOR
Cessandra Dillon

BACK COVER COPY
Laura Pokrzywa

COVER DESIGN
Barb Fisher, LeVan Fisher Design

COVER AND TEXT ILLUSTRATIONS
Greg Call

INTERIOR DESIGN
Ragont Design

PRINTING AND BINDING
Bethany Press International

The typeface for the text of this book is
Centaur MT